Return of a Pig Called Heather

Harry Oulton has worked for Eurodisney in Spain, Coca-Cola in Mexico, made television programmes for both the BBC and ITV, and worked in a factory sticking labels onto boxes. Now he's very happy writing children's books in London, where he lives with his wife and three children. Find out more at www.harryoulton.co.uk or follow him on Twitter @HarryOulton1

The HEATHER series

A Pig Called Heather
The Return of a Pig Called Heather
Heather's Piglets

HARRY OULTON

Piccadilly
PRESS

First published in Great Britain in 2014 by
PICCADILLY PRESS
80–81 Wimpole St, London W1G 9RE
www.hotkeybooks.com

A CIP catalogue record for this book is available from the British Library.

ISBN: 978-1-8481-2473-8
also available as an ebook

1 3 5 7 9 10 8 6 4 2

Typeset in Adobe Caslon Pro 12.5/17pt

Printed and bound by Clays Ltd, St Ives Plc

Hot Key Books is an imprint of Bonnier Publishing Fiction,
a Bonnier Publishing company
www.bonnierpublishingfiction.co.uk

For Poops and numbers 8, 9 and 11

Chapter 1

The Unknown Apple

As the late July sun warmed her back, the pig called Heather rested her snout on her front trotters, yawned and happily swallowed the last of her apple. It had been a good apple, and now that it was inside her she felt stronger and more able to think about things. Trouble was, there were a lot of things to think about and they were all as complicated as each other. Every time she thought one of them was a happy thought, suddenly there turned out to be a sad bit to it as well.

She had come to London and found Isla, her best two-legged friend. That was definitely happy, but it did mean that now she was miles away from Scotland and her beloved farm, and she had no idea whether she'd see her best four-legged friends, Rhona the goat and Alastair the sheepdog, ever again.

She had escaped from the advertising agency that had made her pretend to be a chicken-farming pig called *Busby*. That was good, but also bad because to do it she'd had to tell a lie and run away from a really nice woman called Nikki and her chatty dog, Izzy. She was also now in disguise, which meant being half-painted black and that was a bit odd and sometimes felt a bit stiff and funny.

She was hiding in London Zoo, surrounded by exotic animals she had never even heard of, let alone lived with before! That was scary but, on the good side, being inside the zoo did mean she was safe from Mr Hornbuckle and his dog Thomas, who'd been hired by the advertising agency to catch her and had spread lies about her having swine flu.

Normally, Heather tried to avoid having too many thoughts at the same time. They made her head hurt. But ever since her barn had burned down, Isla had moved to London and Heather herself had become really famous, it had been non-stop. One thought after another, so just when she'd got rid of one there'd be another there to take its place. She couldn't remember the last time her head had been nice and empty.

Crossly, she got to her feet and shook her snout from side to side, hoping everything would drop out of her ears and leave her in peace. The shaking made her a bit dizzy but it seemed to work. There was only one thought left. More of a question than a thought, but it was a question that needed answering.

Exactly what sort of apple was it she had just eaten?

Heather prided herself on her knowledge of apples. At the last count, she knew over eighty different varieties, and she sorted them both by appearance and taste. But this was a new one. She headed over to the very apple tree that was puzzling her, sat down on her bottom and looked up at it. There were plenty of apples dangling welcomingly from its branches and she snouted one of them curiously. It smelt delicious, and as she opened her mouth to chomp it, out of the corner of her eye she noticed a little tag attached to one of the branches. It was faded and quite hard to make out, but as Heather peered at it she could just about see a picture of the apple she had been about to munch, and the writing next to it.

Malus domestica – 'Lady in Red'

Heather had been taught to read by Rhona the goat, but she wasn't expert at it. Those first two words were too big. They didn't even look English. She peered at the next one. Hmmm. She sounded it out just like Rhona had taught her. L-a-d-y. Laddie? Laddie in Red! How excellent. An apple that might have been named for a Scottish Duroc pig! *She* was red, after all. Or she would be when the paint that Isla had used to disguise her had all worn off. She was a lassie rather than a laddie, but never mind. It was a good name for a good apple. She closed her mouth around another one and bit into it. Delicious. Such an interesting flavour. What was it? She sifted through her memory of tastes and eventually tracked it down. Some time ago, Isla and her dad had taken her to a fair and entered her into the 'best pig' competition. She hadn't won, but she remembered Isla giving her some fluffy sweet stuff on a stick. It had got stuck around her snout and Isla'd had to mop it off, but it had been very delicious. Candyfloss, it was called. That was what this apple reminded her of. She snuffled happily at the memory and stored the information away. *Laddie in Red, pink fleshed, candyfloss-flavoured with a good finish.*

Now feeling rather chirpy, she carried on towards the dark entrance to the enclosure. Isla had told her there were bearded pigs inside and, sure enough, as she rounded the corner she saw two little piglets messing about with an orange. They were striped, which she knew meant they were young. As Heather watched, one of them rolled the orange to the other, who expertly flicked it into the air with his snout, waited for it to come down and then flicked it up again and again and again, sometimes snouting it and sometimes flicking it up with his trotter. Finally he casually snouted it over towards the other one, who watched it sail through the air and then, at the last moment, dropped his head and caught the orange on the back of his neck. He flicked it back into the air, caught it again, and carried on with the snouting and flicking until eventually the orange split and burst apart mid-flick, getting juice and pips all over the laughing piglets.

Heather coughed. 'Um, excuse me?'

The two piglets turned to look at her. One of them nudged the other and whispered something, then both piglets giggled and high-fived each other's trotters.

The first one raised his snout to Heather.

'Yeah?'

'Um, hello. My name's Heather. Heather Duroc. I'm from Scotland.'

The two piglets looked at her. The first one said, 'I'm Thom,' and the other said, 'I'm Ramelan,' and then together they both said, 'And we're the wild piglets!' They high-fived each other again happily.

'I wondered if your mother or father was around?'

Thom shouted behind him. 'Mum! Someone wants you.'

A voice from inside said something Heather didn't understand and Ramelan rolled his eyes and turned towards Heather. 'Mum says who are you?'

Heather swallowed. 'It's a bit hard to explain. As I said, I'm Heather. I'm —'

Thom interrupted her and shouted towards the dark doorway again. 'It's a pig. Says her name's, like, Arthur or something.'

The foreign voice came again and the piglet turned back to Heather. He jerked his head towards the doorway. 'She says go in.'

There was a deep, rolling rumble in the sky and the next second Heather felt drops of warm, summer rain starting to splash onto her back. The two piglets snorted in delight and raced for a muddy spot where they started to roll happily. Heather looked at them enviously. She'd always loved summer rain and normally she would have joined them – it was ages since she'd had a really good wallow – but she knew she should go and introduce herself to her new friends. Sadly, she took a last look at the frolicking piglets, let a few final drops splash onto her back, and reluctantly headed through the door.

It was a bit gloomy inside and she could just make out a group of pigs all lying around and chatting. As Isla had said, they did all have skinny bodies with massive heads, and their bearded snouts made them all look very important. The beards reminded her of Rhona, which was good. If they were like her best goat friend then everything would be fine. She took a deep breath and coughed discreetly. Four heads turned round and everything went quiet.

Heather felt all eyes on her. There was total silence and then one of them spoke. 'What are you?'

'I'm Heather.'

'Not *who*. What?'

'I'm a Duroc pig. My name is Heather.'

'Durocs are red. You look like a saddleback. Or maybe a hippo.'

The other pigs laughed at this, and the speaker came over to Heather. His bearded snout jerked at her aggressively and he circled her until she started to feel dizzy.

'Why are you here?'

'I'm hiding. You see I'm not really black at all —'

'You don't say.'

Heather ignored the sarcasm. 'I'm normally red. As you say, Durocs are red and I'm a pure-breed Duroc, but I've run away. I'm in hiding – sort of . . . well, it's complicated, but have you heard of this silly thing, you probably haven't but . . . Busby?'

A sudden indrawn hiss of breath stopped Heather in her tracks.

'Busby,' repeated the pig. Then he turned to the others and said something in a language Heather couldn't understand. There was muttering and the other pigs all got to their feet and came and stood around her in a menacing circle. Heather gulped.

'That's right. I mean, I know it's weird, but I am Busby.' She laughed nervously.

'Busby's red.'

'Yes, well, so am I when I've not been painted black. Honestly, look.' She stood on her hind legs and pretended to be sowing seed, just like she did in the advertisments for Busby's Birds. The pig snarled at her and she dropped down again.

'Busby is famous. Busby is on posters. I think you are a dirty, nasty little mongrel pig who has wandered in here uninvited and unwanted.'

Heather looked around for a friendly face, but they were all a bit daunting and rather frightening. She backed up until her bottom was against the wall. There were now four large bearded pigs all facing her and all looking very unfriendly. The leader spoke again, quieter now.

'I heard Busby'd run away. I heard she was mad. Somebody told me she had swine flu. So, if you're Busby, then you're sick. You know what they do with pigs who've got swine flu?'

Heather shook her head frantically. 'I don't have it! Isla said I didn't have it. She said if I was hungry I must be okay. And I am! Hungry, I mean. I've just eaten one of those nice laddie apples outside but I'm still starving so I'm definitely okay. Definitely! I haven't got anything.' She was frantically turning on the spot, but the bearded pigs weren't listening. They bared their teeth and closed in.

Chapter 2

The Princess
and the Pig

'Stop!'

The command was delivered in a low, flat bark, which seemed to come from the shadows on the other side of the room. The bearded pigs grudgingly backed off, snarling as they went, leaving a terrified Heather quivering against the wall.

'Bring her to me.' Again the voice from the

darkness. The pig who'd been about to attack Heather crossly waved his trotter at the darkened corner.

'You heard him. Go over there.'

Heather reluctantly trotted over to a pile of straw in the very darkest corner of the room. As she got closer, she was able to make out a figure. It was a male pig. He looked about her age, but he was much larger than the others, with a bushier and more splendid beard. When he spoke, his voice was deep and rumbling. It reminded her of the storm cloud, but a bit less friendly.

'Who are you?'

'H-H-Heather.'

'You said you were Busby.'

'Heather's my real name. Heather Duroc. That's what Isla's mum called me when I was a tiny piglet. I used to eat heather, you see, and I'm a Duroc pig so —'

He raised a hoof to stop her. 'Then who is Busby?'

'He's a farmer. Chicken farmer. Busby's Birds. That's why they called me Busby. As an advertising thing to sell more chickens. I think.'

'What are you doing here?' he asked.

'I've run away.'

'Why?'

'It's a long story.'

The pig settled down into the straw and blew out through his nostrils. 'I'm not going anywhere. And unless you'd rather go back and spend time with the others, I don't imagine you are either.'

Heather took a deep breath. She thought for a moment about telling him all about Isla, but why should she? That was her business. It was private. She flopped down, resting her head on her trotters.

'Did I say you could sit down?'

Heather looked at him in disbelief. Was he serious?

The mighty pig snorted crossly. He waved his bearded snout towards the pigs sitting on the other side of the room. 'They were about to kill you until I stopped them. I suggest you show me some respect.'

'Oh,' said Heather.

The pig levered himself to his feet. Standing on all fours, he was even more terrifyingly massive and Heather gulped. He towered above her, his body nearly a metre high. It was ages since another pig had actually made her feel small. He sat back on his haunches which somehow made him seem even taller, and as he spoke, his long, gleaming white tusks twitched menacingly.

'Do you want to know why you are so unpopular? Why your fate was sealed the minute you walked into this room?'

Heather shook her head but he ignored her and carried on. His English was perfect but he had a foreign accent that Heather couldn't place.

'We are the Sus barbatus. Sus meaning pig, barbatus meaning bearded. Of all the pure-breed pigs we are the rarest, the proudest and the noblest. People come from everywhere to see the famous Sumatran and South-Asian bearded pigs. We have the adoration of zoo visitors from all over the world. Our piglets even have stripes! And then what happens? You come along and it all goes out the window. Years of hard-won respect, centuries of culture, breeding and nobility, all destroyed by one ginger celebrity named Busby.'

As he said the name he shuddered, his voice

dripping with distaste and loathing.

'These days all the public ever ask is if there are any Durocs. Nobody is interested in us any more; it's all *Where are the Busby pigs, Mummy?* or *I don't like the ugly beardy pigs, where's the pretty red one?* You want to know why we don't like you? There's your answer.'

Heather was quite scared. Of all the places she could have come to hide, it was just her luck to have picked the one where she was least welcome. But there was something else, too. As she looked at this vast mountain of a pig, this noble giant, the very finest example of her species, she was awestruck, but she was also annoyed. He might be all those things he said, but she was a pure-breed, organically reared Duroc pig! Why should he be more worthy than her? Just because he knew fancy words, that didn't give him the right to speak to her like that. He didn't know her, didn't know anything about her! Angrily, she rose to her feet and stood to face him.

'Get rid of me, then. Destroy what's more famous than you and you'll be top dog again. Come on. I won't squeal.'

It was hard to tell, but she was almost certain the vast pig had smiled behind his beard. Certainly when he spoke there was a different tone to his voice. 'Do you know the story of Scheherazade?'

Heather shook her head. 'No.'

'There was once a rich, cruel king who had everything he wanted. But he was lonely and nobody could make him happy. Every night he called for a different woman, but they were so scared of him they couldn't speak and every morning he would banish them and send them into the wilderness outside his castle. This went on and on until one day it was the turn of a girl named Scheherazade. She told him a story. It was such an exciting story that the king was utterly entranced. Scheherazade stopped the story right at the best bit and said she was tired and wanted to go to bed. The king was furious, but he was enjoying the story so much that he ordered her to come back the next day and finish it. So she did, but then she told him another story and another and another, and every night she would stop at such an exciting point that the king would be desperate for her to come back the next day so he could know the ending. This went on for a thousand and one nights until Scheherazade said she had no more stories, and so she would have to be banished with the others outside the castle walls.'

'And?' asked Heather, curious despite herself.

The giant pig settled down in his straw and arranged his vast body comfortably. He opened his mouth and yawned, his cruel tusks gleaming wickedly as he did so. 'And I'm bored, little Duroc. I have no need of you except to distract me from my boredom. So amuse me. Tell me a story.'

Heather gulped nervously. 'I don't know any.'

'Then make one up.'

So Heather told him a story. The only one she had. About a girl called Isla who lived on a farm with her best friend. Heather told him how happy Isla was as she ran in the fields, skimming stones in the burn, going to pet day at school, and playing with her friend. Then the story took a darker turn, disaster struck and Isla was forced to leave the farm and move somewhere she didn't want to be, with people she didn't know. She'd had to leave her friend behind and now was lost and upset, suffering in the vast prison of the city, longing for the hills and rocks and openness of the countryside, where her heart still ran free. And now the girl and the friend were so saddened by being apart that they both started to waste away. Heather told how the friend had come to find Isla, eventually tracking her down in the jungle of the city and how the two of them had never been happier, until they were torn apart again.

The vast pig was utterly silent throughout, listening intently and not moving a muscle; and when Heather stopped, he raised his head and stared right through her. 'So where is this Isla now? Why aren't you with her?'

'I didn't say it was about me,' said Heather.

The pig grunted, his beard quivering as he spoke. 'Those emotions you describe. You have to feel those to know them. Nobody could tell a story like that if it wasn't about them. Why aren't you with her?'

'Because a man called Mr Hornbuckle is hunting me. I'm hiding here. Isla says I'm safe from him in the zoo.'

The pig nodded. 'She's right. What happens next?'

'I don't know,' said Heather truthfully.

The large pig raised his mighty head and bellowed to the other pigs. 'Thom! Ramelan! Fetch our guest a bowl of water and something to eat.'

The twin piglets appeared a few minutes later, pushing a bowl of water with two apples bobbing in it. Heather hadn't realised how hungry she was and tucked into the apples (*Golden Delicious, the classic apple, crisp and juicy with an almost sugar-cane sweetness*) with gusto. Then she sat back, burped, stuck her snout into the water and drank deeply. In the past she'd never really seen the point of water. She couldn't be certain but she suspected there might actually not be any sugar in it at all. But this bowlful was delicious.

With some food inside her, Heather felt a little stronger and more like herself. She cleared her throat.

'So can I stay? For a bit, I mean. Until Isla tells me where we're going next?'

He stared at her thoughtfully. 'Harbouring a fugitive is dangerous. We could get into trouble.' He paused and then smiled, his tusks twitching. 'I like danger. It makes life so much more fun.'

'So, is that a yes? Only the others didn't seem so…' Heather jerked her head towards the others.

'I will talk to them.'

Heather rolled onto her back and pointed her trotters at the ceiling.

'Why have you got an accent? They haven't.'

'They were born here. That's another reason they're so angry with you. They have all been bred and raised in captivity. It's hard for them when they hear about life outside the zoo.'

'Where were you born?'

'My ancestors originally came from the Basque country, a small region at the top of Spain. Some years ago, there were only twenty Basque pigs left in the world, so my great-grandfather was taken to Borneo and crossbred with the bearded pigs there. Basques are very proud, so in order to preserve our roots, every male calls their first-born son Aitor, a traditional Basque name which means "good father". So, although I was born on the island of Borneo, although I grew up by a schoolhouse listening to the stories and lessons of a teacher who spoke to his pupils in the many and beautiful languages of Borneo, I know that my name is Aitor, and the blood of Basque pigs flows through my veins like an unquenchable fire.'

'Blimey. I'm just a Duroc from Scotland. Nothing fiery in me, I'm afraid. Mind if I have a snooze? Only I'm a bit sleepy.'

She snuggled down in the straw and yawned hugely. 'By the way, did she die?' mumbled Heather. 'Sheherry-thingy?'

Aitor cleared his throat. 'On the one thousandth and first night the girl said she had run out of stories and would have to be banished. The king was horrified, for he had fallen in love with her, so he begged her to stay and be his wife. The girl refused, saying how could she marry someone so cruel? The king promised to change if she would stay with him. Scheherazade agreed, but said if he was ever mean or cruel again she would leave him and join all his other victims outside the castle wall. True to his word, he became the best king the country had ever had, and Scheherazade was his queen for the rest of their lives.'

But Heather didn't hear a thing. She was fast asleep, dreaming about another girl who was very stubborn and never stopped talking. She was dreaming about Isla.

To: Millie Raphael-Campbell
From: Isla Wolstenholme

Hi Millie,
Great to see you at the zoo! Did you get into loads of trouble for helping me break into the zoo and hide Heather?!!! She's really well, and you should see the bearded piglets. So stripy and cute!!! Email me back.
Love Isla
xxxxxxxx
PS How is Miss Stephenson? Was she really cross?

To: Isla Wolstenholme
From: Millie Raphael-Campbell

Hi!
We got into loads of trouble but it was really cool and such fun. I sat next to Tullynessle Morag on the way home and I told her about you sneaking Heather into the zoo but said it was completely a secret and she thought it was really cool!!!
Love Millie
xxxxxxxxxxx
PS Say hi to Heather!

Chapter 3

Friendship is Blind

After her conversation with Aitor, Heather found that things got a lot better. Everyone was more friendly towards her and she started to relax. They decided it would be best if she stayed hidden in the building where they slept, and so she spent her time inside, eating, sleeping and trying not to think about Isla.

Then, after she'd been there about a week, the twin piglets, Thom and Ramelan, came inside where she was chatting to Aitor.

'There's this weird girl outside,' said Thom.

'She's wearing a red football shirt, but it's not Liverpool or Arsenal, or Man U,' added Ramelan, sounding puzzled.

Thom carried on, 'She keeps loudly whispering "Hi there", as if we're going to answer her.'

Heather jumped up. 'Isla! Is she saying "Heather"? That's my name! It's an Aberdeen football shirt. That's who she supports!'

She turned to Aitor. 'Come and meet her.'

The big pig shook his head. 'I'll stay here, I think.'

'Come on! I really want you to meet her.'

'No, I don't want to intrude. You go.'

Heather couldn't be bothered to argue any more so she discreetly poked her head outside to check nobody was looking. She could see Isla standing by the railings, shadowing her eyes from the sun with her hand as she tried to peer in. Heather turned to the twins. 'Get her to go round the back, where that bush is, right by the railings, could you? Please?'

The piglets trotted over to Isla and nodded sideways with their heads until Isla understood and came scampering round the back, to where Heather was hiding in a bush just by the fence. She was jumping up and down so much the bush looked as if it was alive, and Isla immediately started talking even faster than usual, the words bursting out of her like exploding popcorn.

'How's it all going? Are you okay? Your paint's wearing off a bit and your hair's growing out so you'll have to be careful. Have you made friends? It looks like you have, because those piglets came to get you so they must know who you are. They're so cool, with their stripes. Are they friendly? Hey, Nikki came over yesterday. Do you remember her? She's the one who was looking after you when you were Busby and she told me that I should hide you in the zoo and she's really cool and nice. Anyway, she was with that weirdo Mr Hornbuckle who's got the sausage dog and he knows you're in here but he doesn't know exactly where and he can't get in with his dog so there's nothing he can do at the moment but we've still got to be super careful because he's' – she put on a ridiculous Mr Hornbuckle voice – '*going to find that pig if it's the last thing I do*. Anyway, then Dad told him to go away and leave us in peace but Nikki stayed for supper again and she's really nice and she brought her dog Izzy with her, who's quite little and really friendly. Nikki was telling me this really funny story —'

'Iseller! It's lunch now!' called Mrs Maatens, the ancient Dutch lady who looked after Isla when Mr Wolstenholme was at work. Isla waved at her before turning back to Heather.

'Got to go. Mrs Maatens wants me. I wanted to come with Dad because he's a bit sad at the moment so I said we should come here to cheer him up. That made it even worse, though, because he said animals just remind him of the farm and that's what's making him sad. Bit of an oops by me. I'm going to try and go back to the farm for the tattie holidays, see if I can get Millie to invite us. Listen, I'll come back very soon, I promise. Scrunch if that's a plan.'

As Heather scrunched her snout extra hard, Isla grinned at her and then ran off, leaving Heather feeling very happy but sad at the same time.

'Who was that?'

'She talks fast!'

Heather turned to the twins, who had found an old tennis ball and were kicking it to each other with their trotters.

'That's my friend Isla. We used to live on a farm together in Scotland but she had to move here when the barn burned down and then she wrote me a letter so when I got famous and came to London I found her, but now there's this man chasing me so I have to hide in here.'

'Cool.'

'Wicked.'

Heather left them playing and went back inside to see Aitor. 'I wish you'd come to meet her. It's quite weird to see her not on the farm, but she's so funny and she is my best friend apart from Rhona and Alastair – and you, well, you're not really a friend, more of a sort of . . .' She blushed and quickly carried on. 'She hasn't changed at all, except she gets skinnier the more she grows. She says her dad's miserable because he's missing the farm and so she's trying to cheer him up by going back to Scotland for the tattie holidays.'

'Tattie holidays?' asked Aitor.

Heather grinned at him. 'In the old days, the children in Scotland used to get extra time off school to help their parents harvest the tatties in October – that's what they call potatoes. Of course, these days they do it all with machines, but they still get an extra bit of holiday time so she'll be up there. She says her dad's really sad. I wish there was something I could do.'

Aitor yawned, his vast mouth opening like a tunnel. Then he planted his front trotters firmly. 'There is something you can do. You can finish your own story. You can't stay here for ever. So go. Return to Scotland. Get the farm back for Isla and her father.'

'What? My farm? Back from where?'

'In Borneo, when I was growing up, about two hundred of us would gather every year and migrate to the summer grazing lands. Two hundred pigs, on a long walk north through jungles, deserts and over rivers. Boars, sows and piglets, everyone walking as one; hundreds of legs, all moving with the same rhythm, all of us marching to the beat of the same drum. I did nine migrations before I was taken, and I remember them all like they were yesterday. If Isla misses the farm like I miss those migrations, then you have to get it back for her.'

'Hang on a minute. How am I supposed to do that?'

'On my first march I wasn't even a yearling, still had my piglet stripes, but I was so excited I thought I'd explode. The pride of walking side by side with my mother in the midst of this great river of pigs. It was a bad migration, though. The tiger hunted us the whole way. Picked pigs off from the herd like fruit off the ground. It was a fight all the way to the grazing lands, but somehow we made it. My father was everywhere, up and down the line, encouraging us, giving us hope when all seemed lost, carrying the piglets on his back when we were too tired to continue, and all the while reminding us that we were the Sus barbatus, the noblest, proudest creatures to ever walk the earth.'

'That's all very well, but it doesn't answer my question. The farm's hundreds of miles away. How would I even get there?'

'Walk. If you can't walk, you crawl. You do whatever you have to do.'

'But even if I did, I can't just go and ask to have the farm back. What you're saying is impossible. And silly, actually.'

Aitor snorted as his emotions got the better of him. Then he looked straight at Heather and the dark pits of his eyes blazed like fire.

'Every migration has a leader. Someone who takes responsibility, who guides the herd. Protects the other pigs. After my father died I led the migration four times before I was captured. I fought monkeys, I ran from tigers and I hid from humans with their deadly bullets and their silent arrows. I had the weight of two hundred lives on my shoulders, and every time we lost a piglet I had to look that sow and that boar in the eyes and ask them to trust in me and carry on. Every day was another impossible task, another series of insurmountable obstacles.'

'But I can't do those things!' said Heather, feeling very nervous.

Aitor paused, as if he'd suddenly remembered where he was.

'The biggest challenges require the strongest hearts. Getting the farm back for Isla will be the hardest challenge you will ever face, so you must ask yourself, how big is your heart?'

Heather looked at herself in her water bowl. She couldn't see her heart, but her tummy was certainly pretty big.

Isla came again the next week, and again the week after. Heather loved every minute of these visits, but she could see the little girl was still really worried about her father and it was making her desperately unhappy. The day after Isla's next visit, Heather went to talk to Aitor.

'The farm. Isla. Let's do it.'

Aitor smiled at her. 'Good. Now, first thing. How

are you going to break out of here?'

'How are *we* going to break out, you mean.'

Aitor looked sad. 'I'm not coming.'

'What! Why not?'

'It's not my fight.'

'It is now.'

'No it's not.'

'Yes it is.'

'No, it isn't.'

'Is.'

'Isn't!'

'Is so!' Heather stood up and stared at him, her snout twitching with indignation. 'Stop behaving like the piglets. You stand there and give me this long talk about tigers and migrations and big hearts and challenges and then I ask you to do one simple thing and you say you can't. Well you're not getting away with that. No way, José!'

Aitor raised a tusk curiously. 'My name is Aitor. Who is José?'

'No one. It's an expression! It means . . . it means . . . well, it just means you've got to come with me. Please?'

'I'm too old.'

'Nonsense. You're the same age as me.'

'The others need me here.'

'They can come too.'

'I can't come with you,' said Aitor.

Heather was getting cross now. 'You know how much Isla means to me. Are you jealous?'

'Jealous? Of a human? Like the piglets say, as if!' Aitor chuckled, which annoyed Heather even more.

'Scared, then?'

'How dare you!' said Aitor, looking right at her. Actually, looking at her mouth. As if he was looking at her voice, rather than her eyes. He always did it and for some reason it really annoyed her.

'At least look me in the eye!'

The mighty boar turned his back on Heather and strode to the corner of the room.

'Good luck with that,' said a voice in her ear. It was Thom. He and Ramelan had come over and were standing beside her.

'Yeah, Uncle Aitor hasn't left this room, like, ever,' added Ramelan.

'Uncle? Aitor's your uncle? But your name is Thom. And you're Ramelan. Why aren't either of you called Aitor?'

'He's not a first son,' said Thom, pointing at Ramelan.

Ramelan took over. 'Although I am a minute older than him. We had a big brother called Aitor. He and Dad were captured on one of those long walks Uncle Aitor always talks about. They went to a zoo in San Diego or somewhere and —'

Thom interrupted him. 'Mum came here with Uncle Aitor and had us here. Uncle Aitor says it was his fault they were captured so he doesn't deserve to ever leave this room again. Which kinda sucks because he'd be wicked in goal. I mean, look how big he is.'

Ramelan nodded. 'True, but you can't have a blind goalie.'

Heather was gobsmacked. 'Did you say blind?'

The twins nodded. 'I think the humans did it when they caught him. Because he's so big they thought he might, like, escape or fight or something.'

Heather was reeling. How could she not have noticed? 'No wonder he doesn't want to leave. He must be terrified.'

'I guess.' Ramelan paused for a second and then looked appraisingly at Heather. 'You're pretty massive. Fancy going in goal?'

Ignoring this, Heather went into the corner where Aitor was sitting on his own, facing the wall. She sat down next to him and nudged him in an affectionate way.

'I didn't know. Why didn't you say?'

'Not your business. Anyway, now you know you can go off on your little trip.'

'Not without you I can't.'

Aitor turned to face her. 'Eder, I can't see. How on earth am I going to leave the zoo, let alone walk to the farm?'

'You know what's really sweet?' she said thoughtfully. 'The way you can't say my name properly, so you call me Eder.'

Aitor snorted crossly. 'I'm perfectly capable of pronouncing the name Heather, but Eder suits you better. Anyway, I'll slow you down too much if I come.'

Heather grinned. 'Nonsense. I'm going to look after you.'

Aitor snorted. 'You? Look after me?'

'Yes, Blindy, I'll look after you. Well, I'll stop you walking into any trees, anyway.'

'I'd just be a burden for you.'

Heather rolled her eyes, which fortunately Aitor couldn't see. 'Listen, when you used to do your long walks, did you always go to the same place?'

'Yes. We used to spend winter in the forests of Kalimantan and then travel north to the tip of Sarawak for the summer. Sarawak is called *the land of the hornbills*, such a beautiful, peaceful country, if you could have seen —'

'Yes. I'm sure,' interrupted Heather. 'Now remind me. North is the one that's down, yes?'

Aitor reared up in disbelief. 'Down? No! North is up! Always up. It is the direction that defines all others.' He pointed with his trotters as he talked, the excitement rising in his voice. 'The sun may rise in the east, but magnetic north is where the needle on the compass points, and is how we guide ourselves. Four true directions, always the same, always in the same order. North, east, south and west. Never, Ever, Stop Walking.'

'Or, Not Exactly Seeing Well?' added Heather thoughtfully.

Aitor roared with laughter and nudged Heather so hard she rolled onto her side.

'It all sounds quite complicated,' she continued as she got up. 'How do you know which way is which?'

'There are many ways to know – the stars, the moss on the trees. I use instinct. My brain's compass pulls me towards north.'

Heather headed off towards the doorway.

'Good. Because Scotland is north and, as you say, I don't know which way that is, so you're going to have to come along or we're going to get very lost. I'll make sure you don't tread in anything horrid and you can pull us north. Now, can we go and get some food please? I'm starving.'

Chapter 4

Penguins May Not Be Able to Fly . . .

The next morning Aitor called a meeting. There was much curiosity among the herd, not least because Aitor insisted they have the meeting in the open air. It was the first time many of them had ever seen him outside. Heather hid in a pile of leaves and listened as Aitor announced that they were going to break out of the zoo.

'We are going to Eder's homeland. She is embarking on a quest and I have offered her our support. Our journey will take us far to the north. It will be a long, punishing walk, so if anybody doesn't want to come that is fine. Is there anyone who would prefer to stay?'

There was silence among the herd. Heather felt quite touched that these seven pigs were going to help her. Aitor continued.

'The first thing to decide is how we are going to get out of the zoo. As you know, Eder broke in by jumping over the fence, but there was only one of her and she had the help of several small, but lively humans. We must find a different, more secure route out of here.'

He paused for a second while the pigs digested the news and whispered among themselves. Then he carried on.

'As far as I know, apart from a red panda who was being moved to a safari park, no animal has ever escaped from London Zoo. It is a fortress designed to keep us safe, but also contained. We need to work out a way of distracting the humans so that we can not only escape, but also make sure that by the time they notice we're gone we are miles away.'

Ramelan's trotter was up in the air, desperately pushing higher and higher to attract attention. He was jumping up and down, but Aitor was ignoring him.

'He's blind, doofus. He can't see you,' whispered Thom.

'Uncle Aitor! Uncle Aitor!' shouted Ramelan, almost taking off, his trotter was so high in the air.

'Yes, Ramelan?'

'There is an animal that escaped. His name was Goldie. It was ages ago but I heard these humans talking about it.'

'Indeed?' Aitor looked interested. 'Who was this animal, and how did he escape?'

'He was a golden eagle – from Scotland, like Aunty Heather – and he flew off when they were cleaning his cage!'

Aitor chuckled. 'There is an expression, *pigs might fly*, but I assure you it isn't true. If you look closely at your back you will see that we don't have wings, so I'm afraid —'

'Stop being so pompous,' interrupted Heather from under her pile of leaves. 'Tell us more, Ramelan. What happened?'

'Apparently he was free for, like, nearly two weeks. They used all nets and stuff to try and capture him again, even, like, a bird whistle, but he just kept on flying. He even stole a duck from someone's garden. The Queen talked about him and everything. They finally catched him again by tricking him down with food. He was wicked.'

Heather nodded sympathetically. She'd been fooled by that food trick before.

'*Caught*, Ramelan, not *catched*. Is he still here?' asked Aitor.

'I don't know. They didn't say.'

Heather smiled at the boy. 'Well done, Ramelan. Aitor, I think you and I had better go and find this Goldie.'

'Don't know what good it'll do, but if you insist, Eder, we'll go tonight.'

'Can we come?' implored the twins, their little tails spinning with excitement.

'Absolutely not. Don't be ridiculous,' said Aitor.

'Please! You wouldn't even know about him if it wasn't for us! Please? Aunty Heather?'

Heather looked at them. 'Will you be good? And really quiet? Promise?'

The twins nodded frantically, their mouths clamped shut.

That night, Heather and Aitor and the others all gathered by the side of the ditch that divided their paddock from the space where the public walked about. They'd found a plank which they balanced on some stones and stretched across the gap so it rested on the top of the fence. It was quite high, and Heather was really nervous. It seemed ages since she'd stood on Isla's back and jumped into the paddock. She thought about her friend fondly for a minute and that gave her the courage to clamber up onto the plank and walk across it. The ditch seemed a long way below and Heather had to be quite firm with herself when the plank wobbled slightly as she inched across it. Then she was at the other side and jumped down happily. She spotted an apple which had fallen onto the ground and escaped being cleaned up. It was a Laddie in Red, and as she happily munched into the crisp, candyfloss-flavoured flesh, she was transported back to the fair where Isla and her dad had had to tell her she hadn't won 'best pig'. She'd been terribly upset and it had taken all of Isla's skill, and a lot of that funny candyfloss stuff, to make her not feel like a complete failure. It was so sweet and —

'Eder!' hissed Aitor from the other side of the fence.

She jumped and concentrated on helping the twins as they scampered fearlessly across the plank and then bounded down to land beside her. Aitor followed, cautiously but steadily, and soon all four of them were lined up on the other side of the fence, looking through at the others as they pulled the plank back so no passing night keepers would get suspicious.

They agreed to squeal when they got back so the remaining six pigs would know to push the plank out again, and then they were on their own. All alone in the moonlit zoo. They didn't really know where they were going, but they figured they'd ask as they went so, cautiously, and keeping their eyes and snouts open for any sight or smell of a human, the four of them sneaked across the open space towards tiger territory.

Although it was dark, the air was hot and humid, and it was eerily quiet. Normally there was a constant hubbub of animals chatting away and humans going on about how amazing it was, but at this time of night there were obviously no visitors, and most of the animals were fast asleep. A few of the nocturnal ones greeted them sleepily as they went past, but nobody seemed to want to chat. They were plodding along by one paddock and Heather noticed there were four identical, very thin trees in a square. She was thinking how pretty that was and then, suddenly, one of them moved!

'Hello?' came a voice from way up in the sky above her head.

'Aaah! What's that?' squealed Heather.

'Describe him,' whisperered Aitor. 'But quietly.'

'Tall thing with a really long neck and brown —'

'It's a giraffe,' interrupted Aitor. 'Keep moving.'

'They sleep standing up, you know.' Thom grinned.

'And their name means "fast walker",' added Ramelan.

'I bet we're faster,' said Thom and he and Ramelan raced off into the darkened zoo. Heather and Aitor followed, trotting along briskly to keep up with the scampering piglets.

They worked their way further and deeper into the zoo, looking everywhere for the birds of prey. There were a few keepers about, doing maintenance, so they tried to stay in the shadows as much as they could, stopping every few minutes to check there was no one around, and running across the open spaces between the cages. Before they knew it, they were by a large enclosed area of stone and water, and Heather hissed to the twins to pause so they could catch their breath and work out where they were. So far they'd managed to avoid being in the open for any length of time, but now they were going to have to cross about twenty metres of open ground with no cover at all.

Heather explained what they were about to do. It was while she was checking everything was all clear that disaster struck.

The two piglets were looking into the pool area curiously, and then, from around a corner, came a hugely fat emperor penguin who headed over to see what was going on. He was about a metre tall, with a vast, white tummy, black back and a pointy beak which he opened and closed with a clicking sound as he waddled laboriously towards them, rocking from side to side on his tiny little feet.

Up till then, Thom and Ramelan had been really well behaved, but a big, fat, waddling white and black thing was just too much. They both took one look and burst out laughing.

'Oh my! What is he?' gasped Ramelan.

'He's so fat he can hardly walk!' said Thom.

'He must eat loads of seafood,' said Ramelan, raising his trotter.

'Whenever he sees food, he eats it!' finished Thom, as they high-fived trotters triumphantly.

'Boys!' said Heather in her fiercest voice, but it was

too late. The penguin was furious. He stared at the pigs, and then tipped his head back, opened his beak and loudly trumpeted his displeasure all round Penguin Beach.

'Shh – please, shh,' pleaded Heather, but it was no good. Within seconds there were penguins everywhere, all of them hooting at the pigs, making short, angry barks like tractors whose oil needs changing. The noise was terrifying – it was so loud that zookeepers started coming out of their houses in their pyjamas to find out what all the fuss was about. Someone flipped a switch and suddenly Penguin Beach was bathed in lights. The pigs were frozen. Any second now one of the keepers would see them. Heather looked round frantically but she didn't know where she was or where to go. She and the others were completely trapped!

'This way,' said a voice and Heather needed no encouragement. She gave the twins a kick with her front trotters and, making sure Aitor was next to her, she ran towards the voice.

The penguins were still roaring their disapproval

as the pyjama-ed zookeepers tried to work out what was wrong, and Heather and the others fled down a ramp and into a sort of tunnel under a road.

Their rescuer was a bird, who flew ahead of them, leading this way and that, turning left and right as he flew low through the zoo, skimming the ground and then soaring up over bins and benches before flipping completely vertical to get round the corners. Although he was flying amazingly fast, he never seemed to move his wings, preferring to hug the ground and skim dangerously low over objects, then soar up and dive down again.

They raced past what looked to Heather like black and white striped horses, and then towards a fenced off bit of zoo with a barrier across it and *no entry* signs plastered all over it. The bird flew underneath the barrier and then headed straight for some narrow steps leading down.

The pigs followed down the steps and then turned the way the bird had gone, emerging into a long corridor with glass-fronted rooms all along it. Clearly this had once housed animals of some kind, but judging by the dust, it had been disused for a while. As they looked around in wonder, the bird spun over itself, flew back towards them and landed perfectly, right in front of Heather and Aitor.

Up close, the bird was terrifyingly big. He stretched his wings out to their full width of over two metres and shook his feathers majestically. His body was a sort of smoky brown colour, with snowy white feathers on his head and neck and a sharp, hooked, yellow beak. The pigs looked at the bird in wonder, as he closed his wings and stared straight at them, his eyes a clear golden colour with a diamond shaped black pupil. Heather gulped as he tilted his head to one side and clicked his wickedly hooked beak.

'Which one of you hogs is going to tell me what y'all think you're doing?'

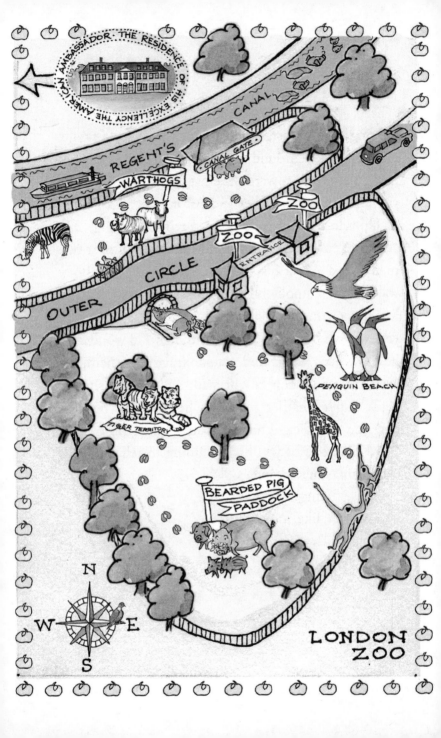

Chapter 5

Fire and Water

The twins couldn't help themselves.

'That flying was awesome!'

'Are you, like, a stunt bird?'

'What's the fastest you've ever gone?'

The bird chuckled and breathed on one of his claws before rubbing it on his feathers so it gleamed in the moonlight.

'Let's see. My cruising speed is usually about forty miles per hour, but in a full dive I can reach a hundred, or thereabouts.'

'No way! That's like a car!'

'How high is a full dive?'

'Three thousand metres, give or take.'

'Is that higher than a house?'

The eagle looked at them, his eyes twinkling. 'You know Big Ben? Tall building with a big clock?'

Thom nodded and nudged Ramelan who quickly followed suit.

'Three thousand metres is a little over thirty – that's *three zero* – Big Bens, one on top of th'other.'

That was almost too much. The boys were momentarily silenced and then Thom whispered to Ramelan, 'He's, like, the best Top Trump ever.'

Talking of open mouths, Heather had spotted an apple core on the ground and she was now dividing it in half. (*Barnack Beauty, a popular cooking apple with a sharp, tart flavour.*) She gave one half to Aitor, who grunted appreciatively and munched the rest to give herself some courage. She felt a bit guilty because her half had been slightly bigger, but only a tiny bit. Aitor swallowed.

'Where are we, Eder?'

Heather looked around her. The bird had stretched out his huge wings and was showing the piglets how he angled and slanted them.

'We're in a bit of the zoo that I don't think they use any more. A bird brought us here.'

'What sort of bird?'

'A big one. With feathers and a beak,' said Heather.

'That narrows it down,' muttered Aitor. 'He sounded American. They're usually friendly, although they do talk a lot. Go and ask him.'

Heather whinnied nervously. She didn't like to admit it, but she was quite nervous. The eagle was very big and more than a little intimidating.

Heather approached the bird and coughed discreetly.

'Um, hello, your um . . . majesty. I'm Heather and these two are Thom and Ramelan, and we live in the zoo.'

The bird looked at her and Heather felt as if he was staring right inside her. In response, her tummy rumbled as it digested the Barnack Beauty. When the

Eagle spoke it was a slow drawl, as if every word had to be rolled around and smoothed in his mouth before it could come out.

'Ma'am; youngsters. Name's Edwin.'

Heather had never been called 'ma'am' before. She quite liked it. 'We, um, wondered if, that is to say – we're sort of looking for someone. A bird, like you. I mean, not that all birds are the same, or even know each other, but I – that is, we – sort of, er, wondered if you knew him, and if you did, whether we could talk to him? I think he's called something like Goldie?'

'Nope,' replied the bird.

'Oh,' said Heather.

'If you don't mind me asking, ma'am, why are you not in your paddock?' asked the bird. 'And, in addition, as you're neither bearded, nor indeed a rare breed, might I ask what you are actually doing inside the zoo at all?'

'She's, like, this really famous celebrity pig called Busby who used to live on a farm with her best friend Isla but there was, like, this fire and they had to sell the farm and move to London and that's when she became all famous and came to find her friend,' said

Thom, before pausing for breath.

Ramelan took over. 'And there's a whole massive army of people searching for her and they're led by this awesome hunter called Hornbuckle and he's got this humongous, terrifying dog but she's safe as long as she's hiding in the zoo.'

The bird put his head on one side and looked at Heather.

'Well, well, the famous Busby. So now you're hidin' here, thereby puttin' everyone in the zoo at some considerable risk. Now that don't seem fair to me. In point of fact, I'd even say it was somewhat selfish.'

'I had nowhere else to go,' said Heather, feeling a bit alarmed.

'Let me explain something to you,' continued the eagle, ignoring Heather. 'This here zoological garden is an extraordinary place. It houses animals from all over the world. I believe something in excess of seven hundred and fifty species. It is well designed and beautifully maintained. Over one million people visit every year, not least because they know we animals are kept in as close to ideal conditions as can be, and are cared for by sensitive, devoted keepers who do everything in their power to simulate our natural, wild environment while also keeping us safe —'

'But it's only a pretence,' interrupted Aitor crossly. 'The animals are not free.'

The eagle looked at him. 'We've not been introduced. Judging by your size, you must be the leader of this little ol' herd? Would that be the case?'

'Eder and I are in joint charge. My name is Aitor.'

'Well then, Aytor, let me enlighten both of you.' The bird clicked his beak again before continuing. 'Animals in the wild face two main threats. Finding food, and being hunted. The vegetarians are subject to the vicissitudes of the weather, while the carnivores must kill to survive, an activity which is both stressful and difficult. The zookeepers provide safety and food, thereby removing both of these problems. They are a sort of benign po-lice, if you will.'

Heather could see the sense in that, but she was curious. 'So why did you save us?'

The bird fixed her with his flaming yellow eye. 'Because if I hadn't, the ruckus would have been terrible.

When the human visitors leave the zoo, everything closes down until the following day. Imagine if the keepers had found four pigs – one of them not even a registered zoo animal – wanderin' around in the middle of the night! That mustn't happen. No, ma'am.'

'*You* wander around in the middle of the night,' commented Ramelan, Thom nodding in agreement.

The bird looked at him. 'I am different. I come and go as I please.'

'How come?'

Edwin puffed out his chest. 'His excellency, the American ambassador, who lives in the large house next door to the zoo, specifically requested I be shipped here from America when he took office.'

'So you're, like, his pet?'

The eagle stared at them, his eyes blazing. 'I am nobody's pet! I am the symbol of Free America and I am here at his excellency's request to ensure, as he does, the protection of the indigenous American citizens, be they animal or human. For that reason, my cage is never locked, and as long as I am habitually available for viewing by the visiting public,

I am free to roam as I see fit, which allows me to nullify any threats that may occur.'

'Threats? What threats?' queried Aitor.

'Some thirty or forty years ago there was an incident involving a bird who broke out of the zoo and ate one of His Excellency's muscovy ducks before he was recaptured.'

'Goldie!' chirped the still-excited twins.

The bird inclined his head. 'Indeed. I am happy to say, since I arrived here there have been no further incidents of that nature.'

Aitor jerked his tusks crossly and his beard quivered. 'Maybe it's not so bad for you because they let you fly wherever you want. For the rest of us, life here is only half lived. I need to feel the grass beneath my feet and the wind in my beard. For us, this zoo is little more than a cage.'

The bird looked at Heather quizzically. 'And yet you're safe here. Forgive me asking, ma'am, but if you'll be hunted down the moment you leave, why do you have such an urge to escape?'

Heather didn't even have to think. 'I want to get

my home back. And to do that I have to get to Scotland. Aitor here can find north, but what we can't do is get out of the zoo. Can you help us?'

The bird shook his head and clicked his beak. 'I'm afraid that would cause too much trouble. If you disappeared they would have to make the cages higher and stronger. It's the animals who would suffer, not to mention the zookeepers who would be sacked for allowing you to escape. I won't be responsible for that.'

Aitor shook his head sadly. 'Then we'll have to do it ourselves. Probably be a lot riskier, cause way more trouble than if we had someone to help us. We'll have to let an animal out of his cage. Escape as everyone runs out of the zoo.'

The eagle clicked his beak. 'When an animal escapes, the zoo goes into lockdown. They can't risk an escape into central London, so everything closes and the humans and animals are all shut inside.'

Thom whispered to Ramelan, who nodded excitedly. 'We'll start a fire!'

Heather went white. She shook her snout but the twins weren't watching. They were both bouncing as they got more and more carried away.

'It's brilliant! We start a fire somehow, probably one of us two, carrying a burning branch and dropping it in some hay or something, then the alarms go off, everything's crazy, everyone runs about, and when the fire engines *neenaw neenaw* into the zoo, we can *neenaw neenaw* out!'

Heather was still shaking her head. She took a deep breath. 'No.'

Ramelan visibly sagged and Thom lay down like a punctured balloon. 'Why not? It's a great idea.'

But Heather had witnessed a fire up close and she knew how terrifying they could be.

'It's too dangerous. Animals get hurt in fires. I won't be any part of it.'

The eagle looked at her and nodded approvingly. Aitor was looking thoughtful. 'What about water? Is there not a canal that runs into the zoo?'

The eagle stretched his wings. 'There is. Boats come down the canal and people leave the boat and enter the zoo through a gate that is situated down by the warthogs. But they close the gate at five-fifteen when the last boat leaves. There's a light and an alarm triggered by movement to stop people breaking in.'

Heather raised a trotter. 'Couldn't you open the gate? We'd be really quick.'

Aitor carried on, 'They'd think you'd set off the alarm, which would give us time to get away.'

But the eagle shook his head. 'I'm afraid, for the reasons I explained earlier, that your leaving the zoo is simply not going to happen. I am prepared to overlook your presence here, ma'am, but I regret I cannot help beyond that. Now, it's getting late, so I would be most obliged if you would return to your paddock forthwith.'

Heather stamped her trotter in frustration. They were so close. Aitor turned round. 'Come on, Eder. We'll just have to let the tigers out and start a fire. Hope too many animals don't get hurt.'

The eagle looked cross. 'That is blackmail. The United States does not negotiate with blackmailers.'

Heather looked sad. 'Then don't negotiate – just help us.' She paused for a second while she tried really hard to remember something that Katy the Eider duck had told her long ago.

'Where's your nest?' said Heather.

The eagle didn't even pause before replying. 'Just above the Anna Ruby Falls on the Chattooga river in the Chattahoochee-Oconee National Park, Georgia, USA.'

Heather turned to Aitor. 'Eagles go back to the same nest every year. Bit like migration. Each year they make it bigger and improve it, but it's always basically the same one. Nest-fidelity, it's called. Katy the duck thought they were bonkers – she always demanded a brand new nest, every year – but I can understand it. Your nest is your home.'

She turned back to the eagle. 'When was the last time you were there?'

The eagle looked away. 'Five years, three months and ten days ago.'

'That's a long time to be away.'

The eagle still wouldn't look at her. 'I am in the service of the ambassador. My place is here.'

'You must really like him. It would take a lot to keep me away from Isla and the farm. I'm sure you can understand that.'

Edwin stared into the distance, then he unfurled his wings and flapped them, creating a wind that ruffled Aitor's beard and reminded Heather of a stiff Scottish breeze. When he spoke, his voice sounded like it was coming from a long way away.

'We'll wait for a night when there's no moon. I'll pretend to be injured on th'other side of the gate. The night keeper will disable the alarm and open the gate, and then you can sneak through while he's checking me over. Once you're through the gate and on the towpath, you're on your own.'

Heather nodded in gratitude. 'Thank you. Would it help if at least one mating pair of bearded pigs stayed here?'

The eagle looked at her thoughtfully. 'Most considerate, ma'am.'

The next moonless night was due in three nights' time, so that's when they arranged to meet. Then they sneaked back to the paddock, oinked to the others to put the plank over and clambered back inside.

That night Heather slept snout to snout with Aitor as he lay in the straw, his sightless eyes staring straight ahead. Heather could hear his massive heart beating inside his chest. A mighty engine which she knew would never fail them, and would carry them forward wherever they went.

'Aitor?

'Hmm?'

'I'm scared. Is this a mistake?'

'Why are you doing it?' asked Aitor.

'For Isla. But I'm going away from her. How will she know where I am?'

'If it is meant to be, then you will find each other.' He rolled over. 'At least you can see where you're going.'

Heather snuggled closer. 'Don't be scared. I'll be beside you every step. Eight legs, one pig. Or something like that.'

'But only two eyes,' said Aitor. 'What if we get separated?'

'We won't. I'm not going to leave you, I promise. Now sleep well. In three days you'll lead the Sus barbatus one more time.'

To: Millie Raphael-Campbell
From: Isla Wolstenholme

Hi!

I've got a plan and I need your help. Thing is, my dad's a bit sad and I think he really wants to come back home to Scotland. Do you remember what fun it was when we did the harvest last year? Why don't you get your dad to ask my dad if we could come to Scotland for the tattie holidays? Think it might cheer him up. Be so cool to come and see you.

Love Isla

xxxxxxxx

PS How are the chickens?

To: Isla Wolstenholme
From: Millie Raphael-Campbell

Hi!
Great idea!! Dad says you've definitely got 2 come for the holidays. It's going to be really big this year because of all the sun so he says it would be great if you and your dad could come. I told him to email your dad so make sure he checks his emails!!!
Love Millie
xxxxxxxxxxxx
PS Chickens cool. Karahi and Biryani both got eaten by the wildcat so we got two new ones called Kiev and Nugget.
PPS Say hi to Heather!

Chapter 6

The Return of
Horatio Hornbuckle

Isla was doing PE with her class when she got called to the head teacher's office. Her heart sank when she went in and saw him with Nikki and Mr Hornbuckle.

'Ah Isla, thank you for coming. Hope you don't mind missing PE?'

Isla was about to answer but Mr Hornbuckle raised his hand to stop her.

'You've been going to the zoo,' he said quietly.

'I like the zoo,' said Isla shakily. 'I go there quite a lot.'

He bent down so he was on the same level as her. When he spoke it was slow and menacing. 'At exactly eleven-fifty p.m. last night, ten minutes before the night keepers changed shift, there was an incident by the canal entrance of the zoo. Anything to say?'

Isla's hand flew to her mouth in genuine alarm. She turned to Nikki, her eyes pleading. Was Heather okay? Mr Hornbuckle watched, and then he turned to Nikki.

'Ms Smith. Clearly Miss Wolstenholme doesn't wish to talk to me. Perhaps you will have more luck?'

Nikki bent down and grinned at Isla reassuringly. When she spoke it was soft and friendly, and Isla relaxed immediately. Somewhere deep in Isla's memory, long, long ago, there had been another woman who talked to her like this, who had a voice like this – soft and loving, but strong and warm. It made her feel safe.

'The zoo's golden eagle seemed to be injured and

was sitting on the ground on the canal side of the fence. The keeper disabled the alarm and opened the gate in order to help him. He couldn't find anything wrong, but as he was checking him over he heard a sound and turned to see the most amazing sight. Six pigs and two piglets, who had clearly escaped from their paddock, passed through the gate left open by the keeper and were sneaking through the grass towards the towpath which runs alongside the canal.'

Isla's brain was whirring as she tried to process what was going on. What about Heather? Was she one of the six? Without thinking about it, she was fiddling with the coin on the string that Heather had found in the field all those months ago and that she now always wore around her neck. Nikki noticed but carried on.

'The keeper sounded the alarm and ran to try and grab them. The moment they realised they'd been spotted, the pigs all ran straight for the canal and jumped in! The zookeeper was in his uniform so couldn't follow them into the water, but he managed to grab one of them —'

Mr Hornbuckle interrupted. 'He did indeed! But, unlike the others, the pig he apprehended was not a bearded pig. Oh no, no, no. In fact, it was not even a registered zoo animal.'

Mr Hornbuckle leant down towards Isla, who was quaking in her PE shorts. His voice dropped again. 'It was a red pig. It had been painted black but, clearly showing through the flaking paint, was the unmistakable red of a Duroc. And not just any Duroc.'

Isla couldn't bear to listen as he stared at her.

'In fact, I'd bet my back teeth that this pig is none other than the missing celebrity pig, your partner in crime – Busby! Am I correct?'

Isla's heart was pounding, but she had to know. She took a deep breath, crossed her fingers and asked the question. 'Did you catch her?'

'So you do know who I'm talking about, then?' asked Mr Hornbuckle quickly.

Isla glanced at Nikki who made a tiny 'no' movement with her head.

'It seems,' continued Mr Hornbuckle, 'that the pig had smeared herself in something, possibly butter, which made it impossible for the zookeeper to keep hold of her. She slipped through his fingers and belly-flopped into the water to join the other pigs. Pigs are surprisingly good swimmers, so by the time we had found a boat and given chase, the pigs were long gone. I sailed up and down the river all night, but they had clearly got out of the canal somewhere and escaped into the park.'

Isla was still worried. 'What about your dog? Couldn't he track them down?'

The pest control operative looked sad. 'Because we don't know where the pigs got back on land, there is no way for Thomas to find their scent. It isn't even clear which side of the bank they used to get out. I will find her, though, never you mind. It is extremely rare for any animal to get the better of me once. No animal has ever done it twice. She won't escape me much longer.'

Isla was relieved but still nervous. She didn't know what on earth Heather was up to, but it sounded like she was safe for the moment. It also sounded as though she had a plan.

Mr Hornbuckle was pacing up and down the head teacher's tiny office. 'Miss Wolstenholme. I rather suspect that this was an inside job. That is to say, those pigs had help. Think very carefully before you answer this question. Where were you last night at eleven-fifty p.m.?'

Well, that was just silly. 'I was in bed. Asleep.'

'Really?'

'Yes! Ask my dad! He stayed up too late watching football so he was really grumpy this morning.'

'I'm afraid I don't believe you.'

The headmaster stood up at this point and cleared his throat. 'You assured me that there would only be a few questions, Mr, um, Hornbuckle, and this seems to be turning into something of an interrogation. I'm not entirely happy proceeding without Isla's father being, er . . . present.'

Nikki looked relieved, but the pest controller wasn't finished. He marched over to Isla and peered down from his full height. His eyes were flashing, but his voice seemed to get even quieter and more menacing.

'And I am not entirely happy at being lied to by a

child who is endangering the animals of London by harbouring a fugitive who is clearly suffering from swine flu!'

'She's not!' Isla couldn't help herself. She was terrified but she had to protect Heather. 'She's fine! I know she is! I asked my dad and he said —' Nikki was making frantic 'shut up!' faces behind Mr Hornbuckle and, mercifully, at that moment, Isla caught her eye and stopped herself in mid-speech.

Mr Hornbuckle was staring at her, his eyes blazing coldly. 'I will give you one last chance to help me, and save yourself a whole trough-load of trouble. As I said, no animal has ever escaped me twice. I *will* recapture her, and you could make it a lot less painful if you told me the truth. It's a simple question. Where are they going?'

'Really, I must protest,' said the head teacher weakly, as Mr Hornbuckle's eyes spat fire at a quaking Isla.

But it was Nikki who stepped between Mr Hornbuckle and Isla. When she spoke, her voice was quiet and calm, but she made it very clear he wasn't to say another word.

'Horatio, stop it. She's only a little girl and you're scaring her.' Nikki turned to the head teacher. 'I think we're finished with Isla – she's free to return to her class now.' The head teacher nodded and Nikki put her arm around Isla's shoulder. 'Come on, Isla, I'll take you back to your classroom.'

As she led her away, Mr Hornbuckle clenched his fists crossly and called after them.

'I don't need your help. I'm going to hunt those pigs down. You mark me!'

As they crossed the playground, Nikki explained that they were all baffled that five of the seven bearded pigs, who'd seemingly always been entirely content and remarkably untroublesome, had suddenly chosen to break out of the zoo the previous night, taking two piglets with them.

'One pair stayed behind. But that's it. And there's another odd thing. What was a Duroc pig doing there?' She looked down at the little girl by her side and a smile hovered around the edge of her lips. 'He thinks it's Busby. As if!' She put her arm around Isla's shoulder, two friends sharing a really good secret.

They reached the main school building and Isla turned to Nikki.

'This is my class, I'd better go in. See you soon, I hope,' she said happily.

'Definitely,' replied Nikki. She bent down and pulled the coin on the string out of Isla's shirt. 'That's a very pretty coin. It really reminds me of someone, but I can't think who. Where did you get it?'

Isla put the coin back inside her shirt and opened the school door. 'My best friend gave it to me,' she said over her shoulder as she raced into her classroom.

At that very moment, the pigs they'd been discussing were settling down in a rubbish dump behind a large building in north London. They'd been running all night and morning so they were exhausted, but really excited.

'That was so wicked!' shouted Ramelan, seemingly still completely full of energy as he and Thom ran about happily.

'Did you see me go into the water?' added Thom. 'I was, like, whoa! There's a keeper, dive!'

'Yeah, and then we were swimming, swimming and the keeper was shouting and then there was this like massive explosion!'

'Yeah, and a huge wave! I thought the keeper had thrown a bomb, but it was Aunty Heather leaping!'

Heather grinned happily at the boys and gave them each an apple to eat. She'd found a load of them in a nearby rubbish bin and was distributing them. *Exeter Cross, red stripes over greenish yellow. Crisp, sweet and juicy.*

'That was a good idea to cover ourselves in butter. How did you know he was going to grab me?' asked Heather between mouthfuls.

'Actually, it was more to protect against the water,' replied Aitor. 'Edwin was worried we might get cold if we had to swim a long way, so I asked him to steal us some butter.'

Heather looked puzzled so Aitor explained.

'It's waterproof. Keeps the water off your skin so you stay warmer. Now I'm going to do a roll call. When I call your name, please answer. Gilbert and Indah?'

'Here!' answered two of the adult pigs.

'Rahmat and Maria?'

'Here!' replied the other pair.

'Thom and Ramelan?'

'Here!' chorused both piglets as they chewed happily.

'Right. Rahmat and Maria, you are in charge of looking after the piglets – stay in the middle. Eder and I will lead the way. Gilbert, you and Indah will bring up the rear. Is that clear? Good. Now it's broad daylight, so we need to hide here and sleep, if we can. We move again tonight – when it's dark.'

'Yessir, Uncle Aitor!' said Ramelan, balancing on his back trotters and saluting with a front trotter before toppling over and landing on Thom.

Heather had finished her first apple and selected a second, chewing slightly more slowly as she wasn't quite so hungry. She was trying to calm down, but there was too much to think about. She was travelling again, and although she was going away from Isla, she was also going home. She took a big bite, and looked around at her friends. There was a buzz of excitement among the band. The escape had gone almost exactly as they had planned it, and they had food in their tummies and somewhere to sleep. Heather felt safe.

Crrrunnch! Mr Hornbuckle bit right through a carrot as he sat in his office, drumming his fingers on the desk. He'd got the CCTV footage of the escape from the zoo and he was watching it over and over for clues. At the moment, the picture was frozen on Heather, flying through the air, eyes squeezed shut and legs pointing out like a starfish, seconds away from belly-flopping into the canal.

Mr Hornbuckle tapped the end of the carrot on his teeth as he stared at the screen.

'Thomas!' he called, and the sausage dog waddled over to where his master was sitting.

'This,' he gestured towards the screen with his carrot, 'was a coordinated escape from the zoo. They had a reason to break out, which suggests to me that they have somewhere to go. The little girl clearly knows nothing, so we need to think like pigs. Work out where they want to end up, and we can work out how they're going to get there. They turned right when they left the zoo which suggests they are going in a northerly direction.'

He got up and walked over to a map of Britain on his wall. Then he placed a pin in the north bit of London and stepped back.

'Information's what we need, Thomas. We must keep reading the papers, listening to the radio and checking the internet for any sightings of pigs, anywhere in the south east. Once we know the direction they're taking, we can work out their average speed and where they're ultimately headed. And then, we can pounce.'

He smiled wolfishly, and stepped closer to the map. 'I'm going to find you, Busby – wherever you are.'

Chapter 7

Heather's Merry Men

'S-H-E-R-W-O-O-D,' spelled Heather laboriously. It was the middle of the night, it was pouring with rain, and they were all standing by the side of the motorway, getting drenched as Heather read a green road sign and the rest of the small herd listened attentively.

'S and H makes a *sh* noise, you know, like in "Shush, Ramelan!"' said Ramelan.

'And W-O-O-D makes *wood* which is like "Would you please be quiet, Thom?"' added Thom happily.

'*Sh-er-wood* – that does sound familiar. There's loads of trees everywhere. Hope some of them are apple trees, I'm starving.' Heather turned to Aitor. 'Isn't there a word for a big lot of trees?'

Aitor shook himself to try and get rid of some of the water on his back.

'In the rest of the world it's sunny in August. Does it always rain in this miserable country of yours? It hasn't stopped since we left the zoo. And yes, the word is *forest*, Eder.'

Something clicked in Heather's memory. 'That's right! Sherwood Forest! Isla used to talk about it. I remember now. Someone really famous lives here. Robin Riding Hood or something. And no, it doesn't always rain in my lovely country. Sometimes it snows.'

Everyone was exhausted. It was nearly morning and they'd been walking all night but Aitor wouldn't let them rest. It was two weeks after the escape, and they were covering a lot of distance, because every night Aitor was the same, driving them onwards, chivvying them to keep going and urging them to put as much distance between themselves and London as possible. Heather was a bit alarmed to see that she was losing weight. She wasn't used to this kind of effort.

'Eder. How far north are we? From London? Where is this Sherwood?' asked Aitor.

'You mean are we nearly there?' replied Heather. 'You sound like one of the piglets.'

Aitor snorted and set off again but Heather had had enough. She lay down and Aitor, sensing that she wasn't by his side, turned back.

'I'm here,' she called. 'Lying down,' she added.

'Then get up. We've got to keep going.'

'Why?'

'Because we've not found anywhere to hide for the day.'

That seemed quite reasonable but Heather was suspicious. 'So if I find somewhere safe for us to sleep you'll let me stop?'

Aitor nodded grudgingly.

As soon as they were well inside the forest, Heather found a nice pile of leaves and flopped down.

There was a beautiful crispness to the air and a lovely damp smell of moss and wet grass. She loved being back in the countryside after those weeks stuck inside the zoo. Feeling the gorse and the leaves under her trotters, watching the butterflies flitting about, rolling in the golden red leaves of the birch and rowan trees, and listening to the night calls of the owls and the nightjars. There were still no apple trees, though. It felt like for ever since she'd had an apple. Aitor kept making her eat acorns, which were okay, but how she longed for a really juicy Magnum Gala, or a lovely crisp Rosemary Russet. Thinking about it made her feel even more hungry and she lay on her back and groaned while trying to ignore how much her trotters ached.

When Aitor joined her, she rolled back onto her tummy. 'I'm exhausted and really hungry. I'd eat my own trotter if it didn't hurt so much. Can we have a day off walking?'

'You can rest when we get there. Now answer my question. How far have we travelled?'

'Does your clever north-detector not tell you that?'

Aitor snorted. 'May I remind you that if I weren't leading you north every night, you would probably still be in the canal.'

Heather grinned. 'All right, keep your beard on. I'm not very good at reading names but I think we're sort of nearly halfway there. There's one of those big blue signs that says *Newcastle and The North*, so I think we should follow that.'

'So, once we get past New-castle we should nearly be at your Old-castle?' chortled Aitor.

Heather looked at him and groaned. 'That is the worst joke you've ever made.'

'Newcastle's awesome!' interjected Ramelan.

Thom nodded in agreement. 'It's, like, a really big town with a wicked football team. They have this, like, massive fan base but they haven't won anything for ever.' He raised his trotter and Ramelan gave him 'respect' with his own trotter before carrying on.

'They play in black and white. Stripes, like us.'

Heather grinned at them. Aitor coughed.

'You two go and find us some food. I've got to talk to Eder.' As the two piglets ran off, Heather called after them, 'Please, no more acorns!' She turned back to Aitor, who was looking serious.

'Right, pay attention. Can you see a bright star up in the sky?'

Heather rolled onto her back and looked upwards. The night sky was a black cushion, covered all over with loads of tiny pinpricks of silver, some bigger than the others, but all twinkling and sparkling above her. It was an amazing sight and, for a moment, she was silent, just gazing in wonder.

'Well? Can you see it?' grunted Aitor.

'What exactly should I be seeing?'

'Polaris. The North Star.'

'Is it sort of silver? Shiny? Small?'

'Yes. It's actually much bigger than the sun but it's so far away it looks like a small twinkly thing. Can you see it?'

Heather gazed up at the sky. Everywhere she looked there were shiny, small, twinkling things.

She crossed her trotters, took a deep breath, and lied. 'Yes.'

'Sure?' asked Aitor.

How did he know she was fibbing?

'Okay, I can't. Well, I probably can, but there are loads of silver shiny things. Which one is your one?'

'It's bright – the brightest star in the sky.'

Heather looked again. There was one star that was much bigger and brighter than the rest. She breathed a sigh of relief.

'Yeah. Got it.'

'So, now you look straight up, and you draw a line between straight up and the North Star. That line is due north. Now you can always find where you are and where you are going. With that line ahead of you, you know that east is to the right of you, south is behind you and west to the left. Okay?'

Heather had absolutely no idea what he was talking about. She remembered the whole north, south, east, west thing, but lines and stars? She shook her head and felt a bit stupid. On the horizon she could see the pink smudge of dawn, flowing upwards as the sun rose, slowly rubbing out the night as it came. Suddenly she thought of something.

'Ha! What if it's the daytime? What if I can't see

your funny star? How do I know where's north and whatnot?'

'Well, obviously in the day you would use the moss on the trees and the direction the flowers grow. Yes?'

Heather stayed silent. Aitor shook his head in disbelief.

'You've lived on a farm all your life. How can you not know this?'

'I know useful things,' said Heather. 'For instance, I can tell the difference between over eighty different types of apple; Pippin, Annie Elizabeth, Foxwhelp, the Hawkeye Delicious, the King David, the —'

Aitor dismissed her with a wave. 'The only apple worth eating is the Goikoetxea. It's from Spain. Makes excellent cider. The apples you grow here are bland and forgettable.'

'Rubbish!' Heather was furious, but Aitor raised his trotter to shush her.

'The easiest way to know where you are going is to use the sun itself. It rises in the east, so until midday if you have the sun pointing at your right shoulder, then you are heading north. Got it?'

Heather was still cross with him for being so rude about British apples so she stuck her tongue out at him.

'Eder, it's important you know how to get home. What if there's a time when I'm not here?'

At that moment, they heard a loud squealing and yelping and the two piglets appeared, out of breath and giggling. Thom was carrying a loaf of bread in a plastic bag and Ramelan was laughing so much he almost couldn't get his words out.

'That was wicked! There was this group of humans having breakfast and they were doing something with the fire, so I went over and the children saw me and they totally loved me and came over to stroke me and then the mother was all like, "Be careful, darlings," and the dad as well and he had a camera so then I, like, stood up – you know, on my back legs – and while they were all looking at me and my stripes and they were filming me, in the back all the time Thom was sneak sneaking and he nicked their bread! So then I ran away and then they saw their food had gone and they totally tried to chase us but they were laughing too much! You should have seen it! We rocked!'

Thom had dropped the bag of bread onto the ground so he could join in. 'Because we figured that I know you don't like us to steal, but these people had loads of food and we don't have any so they didn't really need it. It was like they were rich and we were poor, so stealing from them wasn't so bad.'

Aitor wasn't happy. 'Just like your grandfather!'

'What? What've we done?' asked Thom.

'You've put us all in danger! They'll know we're here and they'll hunt us down!'

'We only stole some bread,' said Ramelan grumpily.

'Anyway you told us Grandad was a hero. You said he saved the herd,' added Thom.

Aitor was still quite cross. 'Your grandfather was a thief. One of the best I ever saw. He could take fruit from monkeys, eggs from birds' nests. Once I even saw him steal a fish from a hawk!'

'So?' asked Ramelan.

'He thought he was invincible. One night, in the middle of a migration, he walked right into a human village and stole a mango from inside a hut.' He paused for a second as he remembered. 'The guard dog saw him, started barking and woke everyone up. Your grandfather fled into the forest but the humans chased him, and to avoid all of us being captured, he had to run away from us. He led the dogs and the humans away, but we never saw him again.'

'But that's really brave!' said Thom.

'It's not brave, it's stupid! It was a mango! He could have got one from a tree, or anywhere, but that wouldn't have been exciting enough. He had to go and steal one from humans. I lost my father for the sake of a mango. Sometimes, Thom, discretion is the better part of valour.'

'What does that mean?' asked Ramelan. Heather was a bit relieved that for once it was someone else who didn't understand.

'It means that sometimes, rather than taking daring risks, it is better to be careful and think before you act.'

Grumpily, Aitor walked off, lost in his thoughts.

'Oops,' said Thom, trying not to giggle.

Ramelan grinned at Heather. 'It was funny, though.'

And he was right. It was funny. So funny that the humans called the film *The Robin Hood Pigs* and put it on YouTube. Within days it had gone viral and was being emailed around as it got hit after hit after hit. Everyone loved the funny film of the stripy, bearded piglet dancing on his hind legs and then scampering off once the other one was spotted stealing the loaf of bread. It was becoming an internet phenomenon and it wasn't long before Isla overheard someone talking about it and logged on excitedly. She couldn't see Heather but bearded pigs running about on the loose must be something to do with her friend. She watched the film over and over again, and thought of Heather being out there somewhere, and that made her very happy, but a bit sad at the same time.

Unfortunately, Aitor was right to be alarmed. Because someone else came across it as well. An email arrived at the computer of Horatio Hornbuckle with a note saying *Thought you might be interested in this*. It sat there for a day before he got round to opening it, but when he did, the effect it had on him was spectacular. He leapt out of his chair, spilling tea everywhere and shouting, 'Sus barbatus!' Then he ran to his car, headed for the A1 and three hours later was in Sherwood Forest. Finally, he had Busby in his sights.

To: Millie Raphael-Campbell
From: Isla Wolstenholme

OMG! You have got to check Robin Hood Pigs on YouTube!!! You know I told you Heather's run away with some bearded pigs and two piglets? They're in Sherwood Forest! They must be coming back to Scotland! Keep an eye out for them! Dad's going to take me out of school for when we come up to visit you. Holidays are different in London so he's talked to my teacher!!!!

Love Isla

xxxxxxxxxxxxxxx

PS How are Nugget and Kiev?

To: Isla Wolstenholme
From: Millie Raphael-Campbell

LOL! That's amazing!!!! Just watched it!!! Those piglets really are awesomely sweet!! I'll def keep an eye out for her but it's a long way from Sherwood to Scotland so she probably won't get here for a bit. Hope she doesn't get captured! School's okay but Kirsty's got into the pipe band final so she's <u>so</u> boasty! Amazing news! We're doing healthy eating at school and we're going on a school trip to your old farm to see round Mr Busby's factory!!
Love Millie
xxxxxxxxxxxx
PS The wildcat got Nugget and Kiev. Dad says he's going to wait with a gun, like Boggis, and Mum says she's running out of names! The new ones are Coronation and Drumstick.

Chapter 8

The Hunt
Is On!

Mr Hornbuckle sniffed the late afternoon air and looked around him. He'd left London three days ago, and he and Thomas had been closing in on the pigs ever since. He knew he was close now, and that it was time to continue on foot. He whistled to Thomas and started to load equipment into his rucksack – a compass, some binoculars, a large net and then a high-powered tranquiliser-dart rifle, accurate up to two hundred metres. He was glad he had Thomas with him. To be honest, the life of a professional pest control officer could be a lonely one at times, and a dog by his side gave him someone to talk to. But now they were on the last leg of the chase. The final section of the hunt, when the two of them worked together like a silent machine. He bent down and adjusted the dog's collar.

'Ready, Thomas?'

The dog looked back at him, his eyes bright and alive. Mr Hornbuckle could see the hunter in there, and he proudly held the dog's muzzle in his hand.

'Usual system. We'll find their sleeping place, you circle round the back and then chase them into this.' He held up the net and shook it.

The dog yapped once, his stumpy tail twitching eagerly.

Mr Hornbuckle reached into his pocket and pulled out a test-tube. It contained a single, red hair, which glinted and glowed as he held it up to the light. Very delicately he extracted it and held it to Thomas's nose. The dog sniffed at it and immediately pinned back his ears and started to quiver.

'It's an interesting smell, isn't it? Sort of warm and milky? No?'

The dog looked at him plaintively and Mr Hornbuckle finally took pity.

'Go.'

After an hour of stalking, the dog sat down on his haunches and waited for the tall man to catch up.

'That close, are we? Excellent. Led me a bit of a dance, this pig has. I'll not lie to you, it's been interesting at work. Some of the boys have been jealous of this one. Plenty of chat in the office, yes indeedy.'

What Mr Hornbuckle didn't share with the dog was the humiliation he'd suffered because of Busby. How the other pest controllers had laughed at him because of his inability to catch one solitary pig. How they'd mocked him, leaving plastic pigs on his desk and making snorting noises every time he went past. 'Could you get me a pork pie, Horatio? Oh no, you can't find them, can you?' Well, he'd show them. Just wait until he returned, with Busby on a leash. Then they'd eat their words. He cocked his rifle, picked up a net and set off towards the wood where his quarry were sleeping.

Aitor was fast asleep, nose to nose with Heather, when Ramelan and Thom woke him. Because they were still only piglets they stood watch together, keeping each other company and keeping each other awake. Now Thom whispered in Aitor's ear that there was 'like, a man with a dog' approaching the wood. Aitor was wide awake in seconds. He nudged Heather and told her to assemble the others. Very quietly they all tiptoed out of the wood.

So, when Mr Hornbuckle plunged into the trees expecting to find the sleeping pigs, it was empty. He was furious and, whistling for Thomas, he ran after them. When he emerged on the other side of the wood he could see the herd of six pigs in the distance – Gilbert and Rahmat carrying the piglets on their backs – and all cantering away across the field.

Throwing caution to the wind, he set off after them as fast as he could run, his dog by his side.

'There she goes, that's our girl, red as a lobster! Next to that big beggar. Snakes alive, he's enormous!'

'He's seen us!' called Thom cheerfully. He and Ramelan were both facing backwards so that they could keep an eye out.

'He's fast,' added an impressed sounding Ramelan.

Heather was scared. This wasn't a game. This man was really chasing her. She was being hunted.

Mr Hornbuckle's legs whirled as he tore after his prey, the wind making his eyes water as it whistled through his moustache.

Heather's lungs were on fire. She was gasping for breath as she galloped up the hill, Aitor encouraging her as he raced along at her side. Occasionally she'd glance backwards, but Mr Hornbuckle just seemed to be getting closer and closer. She skidded as she reached the top of the hill and was confronted by an amazing sight.

It was as if they were standing on top of the world. Under their feet, the hill dropped steeply, falling away as it descended towards a huge pit at the bottom. Heather thought a giant must have come with a massive spoon and taken a huge scoop out of the land. She caught her breath.

'Wow.'

Aitor was at her side. 'What is it, Eder? What's wrong?'

'Nothing. It's amazing. Like Isla's sand pit. But much, much bigger.'

'I'm sure it's very nice, but aren't we being chased?' said Aitor.

Heather jumped. 'Yes! Course! But everyone – be careful, this hill is steep.'

They set off down the hill, scrabbling and scrambling to avoid falling down the steep slope.

'Look, a door!' shouted Ramelan.

Heather turned to look and, sure enough, there was a boarded-up entrance leading into the side of the hill.

Aitor skidded to a halt.

'Can we get in?'

'It's blocked, but I'm sure we could squeeze through.'

'Perfect! Rahmat, you and Maria keep running and draw him away. Gilbert and Indah, go away from us towards the big sand pit Eder was talking about.

Meet up at the bottom. We'll hide inside until the man's gone. We'll catch up with you later!'

Then he and Heather turned and scrambled back towards the old boarded-up doorway.

On the other side of the hill Mr Hornbuckle increased his speed. He was moving faster than he ever had before, his legs a blur as he powered up the hill, desperate to regain sight of the pigs. He paused for a second and checked on Thomas. The little dog was racing behind, his small, stumpy legs going as fast as they could.

Heather and Aitor were at the door. It was the entrance to a tunnel into the side of the mountain, and it obviously hadn't been used for a long time as it was covered in signs saying *Keep Out!* and *Danger!* Boards were blocking the entrance but they seemed old and rotten. She was sure they could get through. She kicked at the boards frantically and felt one of them come loose.

Mr Hornbuckle reached the top of the hill and scanned the ground below him. Dawn was breaking, the sky getting lighter as the sun clambered towards the horizon and, below him, he could see pigs running, two of them with piglets bouncing on their backs. He dropped to his knees and reached for his gun.

Heather was urging Aitor through the hole in the boards, but it was too small!

'Aitor, push!' she whispered. 'But quietly. And hurry!' Between them, they forced at the planks, desperately wriggling, trying to make the hole bigger. They pushed and pushed and suddenly Aitor shot through, breaking the plank and landing in a heap inside. They'd made it!

Mr Hornbuckle opened the breach of his gun and selected a tranquiliser dart. It was powerful enough to knock out a bull, so he reckoned it would certainly be strong enough for Busby. He slid it in and closed the rifle with a solid *thunk*.

Heather was following Aitor inside when suddenly her snout was filled with such a powerful smell that she was nearly knocked over. It swamped her and left her gasping for breath. But it wasn't a bad smell. Quite the reverse. It was the unmistakably sweet scent of one of Heather's favourite apples – *Spartan, deep red skin with a pineapple taste and crisp, white flesh.*

Mr Hornbuckle put his rifle up to his shoulder. He put his eye to the telescopic sight and scanned across the line of fleeing pigs; one and two, both with piglets clinging on; three, four, and then . . . nothing. He scanned back the other way. Four pigs and two piglets. Where were the other two?

Heather was frozen. It was days since she'd had an apple, let alone a Spartan. Slowly she turned her head to see where the smell was coming from. Her mouth filled with saliva as she saw, not ten metres from the tunnel entrance, a ridiculously heavily-laden apple tree. Its branches were groaning with the familiar dark red fruit. On the ground were scattered windfalls, some of them bruised, some of them split, but all of them, undoubtedly, delicious.

Mr Hornbuckle lifted his rifle again and stared through the telescopic sight. Slowly he started to turn to the left as he panned deliberately around the landscape, covering everywhere as he carefully set about locating the missing pigs.

Heather knew she should run, but she could see the apples. They were so close! If only they'd been cookers – Alexanders or Woolbruck Russets – then she could have ignored them. But nobody could walk away from a Spartan.

Mr Hornbuckle was turning slowly, his gaze getting closer and closer.

Heather was in agony. She had to be strong. Or did she? The man was turning towards her, but he hadn't seen her yet. If she was quick she could do it. She knew she could. She leant inside.

'Aitor! One minute.'

As the sun finally rose over the horizon, bathing the whole world in a golden light, Mr Hornbuckle's slowly-turning telescopic sight was suddenly filled with a huge, red bottom. He reared back and dropped the gun but, when he looked back, what a sight met his eyes.

There was a doorway leading into the mountain, and about ten metres from it was an apple tree. Sitting there, right in the middle of the windfalls, oblivious to everything but her stomach and shaking with happiness, was Busby.

This was too good to be true. Mr Hornbuckle dropped to one knee, lifted his rifle to his shoulder and looked again through the telescopic sight. The pig jumped into focus and he got his first really good look at her. The black paint was all gone now, and she was an amazing flaming red colour – the hairs on her skin glowing in the sunlight – and she looked more beautiful than he'd ever imagined. He glanced at his watch: 5.46 a.m. Slowly and quietly, he took the safety catch off his rifle, held his breath and flexed his fingers as they closed around the trigger.

In her bedroom in London, Isla suddenly sat bolt upright. She put on her slippers and padded through to her dad's room. She shook his shoulder.

'Dad! Dad!'

He woke up, gazed at her blearily, reached for his glasses and looked at his alarm clock. It read 5.46 a.m.

'It's the middle of the night. What's wrong?'

'Something's happened to Heather. I know it.'

Mr Wolstenholme flopped back on his pillow. He took his glasses off and put them on the bedside table.

'Try not to think about it, love, or at least wait until it's getting-up time.'

Mr Hornbuckle closed his left eye and aimed directly at the very plumpest bit of Busby's wobbling bottom. Slowly and deliberately, he squeezed the trigger, and with a quiet whoosh, the dart shot out of the gun.

Chapter 9

What's Mine
Is Yours

Heather groaned. She was bruised and battered and
had no idea where she was. Her whole body ached
and her front right leg in particular felt very hurty.
What had happened? The last thing she remembered
was eating a delicious Spartan apple. More than one,
actually. She remembered thinking that even Aitor
would have to admit how delicious this apple was,

and that made her feel guilty, so she'd picked up the nicest one she could see and set off with it in her mouth to take to him.

Where was that apple now? Then it all came flooding back. She had just turned around and was having to be really strong-willed not to eat Aitor's apple, when she'd heard a sort of whoosh and seen a pointed thing flying towards her incredibly fast.

Before she had time to get out of the way, the pointy thing hit Aitor's apple with a loud thwack! She looked up the hill to see what had attacked her, and there was Mr Horn-thingy staring right at her!

They'd locked eyes for a second and then he'd jumped to his feet and started running towards her. That had sparked Heather into life, and she'd set off for the door as fast as her trotters would carry her.

The trouble was, Mr Hornbuckle was running downhill, and Heather was running up. Even galloping her fastest, there was no way she was going to get to the door before he did.

Mr Hornbuckle was closing in. She was pretty quick, he had to admit, but he was quicker. His feet were struggling to go fast enough, and sensing he was within range, he took three last steps and leapt.

Heather looked up to see the wild face of the pest controller, moustache flattened, arms outstretched, flying through the air towards her. Heather tried to dodge, but she'd never been a particularly fast turner, and she lost her balance and skidded sideways, going head over heels. As she did, she saw an anguished Mr Hornbuckle fly past, scrabbling at her skin as he did so, only to feel his clutching fingers latch onto and grip her curly tail.

Heather squealed with surprise and pain, planted her trotters and yanked her bottom forward. Fortunately, it was enough – her tail slid through the huntsman's fingers and the freed Heather ran for the doorway and leapt inside, followed only by an anguished cry and then a series of *bump*, 'Ouch!' *bump*, 'Oof!' *bump*, *bump*, *bump*, 'Oooooh!' sounds as the pest controller rolled uncontrollably down the hill like a bouncing football. Down, down, down, until finally the bumps went silent and were replaced by a long howl and then at last a loud splash as he rolled over the edge of the cliff and plummeted down to the bottom of the water-logged quarry.

Unfortunately, Heather was going quite fast and, just at the moment she'd leapt, Aitor had popped his head out to find out why she wasn't with him. There was a mighty crash, both pigs went head over heels and themselves rolled down and down a sloping corridor until they reached a hole in the tunnel floor which also went straight downwards.

They fell down and down and down once more for what seemed like ages before, finally, Aitor landed in a big pool of mud with a massive squelch and Heather landed . . . on Aitor.

'Oooof!' The air whooshed out of him as Heather landed smack on top of him and lay there wriggling, with her trotters in the air.

So here she was, in pain and groaning, with no sound from underneath her.

'Aitor? Where are you? What happened? Where are we? My trotter hurts and it's really, really dark and . . . are you okay?'

'I'll be fine . . . once you get off me.'

Heather rolled off him but she didn't go too far. It was very dark.

'What were you doing? What kept you?' asked Aitor as he picked himself up.

Heather remembered. 'There were apples! Spartans! They're almost my favourite. Look, I brought you one,' said Heather, realising then that in all the excitement she must have dropped it. Quickly she changed the subject.

'Why is it so dark in here? And, actually, where are we?'

'Smells like we're deep underground. Probably a mine. Where humans dig for things.'

'Dig for things? Like in a garden? What things?'

'Coal, tin, even salt.'

Sometimes Heather felt so ignorant. Aitor was like Rhona. They both just seemed to know so much.

'Why do they dig for it? Is it food?'

'No. It's mostly for power. They burn coal in a big furnace. A huge fire.'

'How do you know these things?' asked Heather in awe.

'One of the zookeepers used to listen to Radio Four, very informative. Knowledge is power, Eder, remember that.'

Heather nodded in what she hoped was a wise way. Aitor obviously couldn't see, so he carried on.

'So, the fire makes steam, and that turns a wheel —'

'Like a windmill!' interrupted Heather in excitement.

'Yes,' said Aitor, in amazement.

'Don't sound so surprised. I'm not completely stupid.'

'Stupid enough to be so distracted by your stomach that you make us both fall down a lift shaft into a disused mine.'

'It was your idea to come in here!'

'To hide! Not to get caught scoffing apples! How many did you eat, anyway?'

Heather blushed in the dark. 'One or two. Or six.'

Aitor snorted. 'Six! So now I'm stuck in the Underworld with Persephone!'

'Will you stop calling me names! I'm not Eder, or

Scheherazade or even Perpersy! My name is Heather!'

'Persephone,' said Aitor gently.

'Who is she, anyway? Actually, don't answer that, it'll be another one of your stories that I feel stupid for not knowing and then there's always a lesson about how I should be thinner, or nicer to people or braver or something. If I'm being perfectly honest, I'm getting a bit fed up of them.'

Aitor ignored her. 'Persephone was the daughter of Demeter, the Greek Goddess of the Harvest. Persephone was so beautiful that Hades, the God of the Underworld, fell in love with her and kidnapped her. He took her down to the Underworld and kept her prisoner.'

'So she was pretty?'

'Very. Prettiest woman in the world.'

Heather grumped. That was better, but he wasn't forgiven yet. 'Didn't anyone notice she'd gone?'

'Yes, and her mother – remember, she was the goddess of crops and the harvest – was so upset that all the plants started to die. So Zeus – he was the main god – realised he had to do something or all the humans would stop believing in him. So he sent his son down to the Underworld to bring her back.'

'Where is the Underworld?'

'Under the world. It's the kingdom of the dead. A place of pain and suffering without light or hope.'

'Oh. So did he get her back?'

'Sort of. You see, everyone knew that if you ate anything while you were in the Underworld then you'd never be allowed to leave, so Persephone didn't eat anything.'

Heather gulped. 'How long for?'

'She lasted a whole month, but after that she was so hungry she ate six pomegranate seeds.'

'That's nothing!' said an appalled Heather.

'Enough, though. They had to do a deal. Every year Persephone spends six months in the Underworld. One month for every seed she ate. In the autumn she goes down there and her mother is so sad she lets all the crops die and throughout the winter nothing grows. Then, in the spring, Demeter makes everything come alive again so that it'll be looking happy and bright for when her daughter comes back and spends the summer on the earth. It's why we have seasons.'

'And then she could eat whatever she wanted?'

Aitor smiled in the darkness and Heather could hear it in his voice. 'Yes, Eder, Hades loved her so much he gave her all the apples she could ever possibly eat.'

'Now you're just being silly,' snuffled Heather. 'Everyone knows apples don't grow underground.'

Heather tried to look around but it was hopeless. She couldn't see anything. It was utterly, totally, completely black. That made her panic, and she turned and turned and was starting to get very tense when she felt Aitor pressing her down to the ground. He sat next to her and gently but firmly put his trotters around her so she couldn't move and felt safe.

'It's only darkness, Eder, don't be afraid of it.'

'But I can't see anything, it's horrible.'

'Close your eyes.'

She did and, annoyingly, it helped.

'Better?'

Heather's eyes were tightly squeezed shut.

'Yes,' she said in a clipped voice, 'but I'm scared if I open them again I'll panic.'

'You'll be fine. It's about balance and control. Your eyes can't see the horizon so you can't balance. If you shut your eyes your body will find its own balance, and you won't be afraid of the darkness any more.'

'Then what?' she asked.

'We look for a way out,' came the steady response.

'But how? Unless you can use some of your fancy coal to make some electricity and light us a path, I think we're a bit stuck.'

'Shall we just stay here, then?'

'Don't be horrid! It's dark, I can't see a thing and it's frightening! If I can't see, I can't do anything. I'm completely useless and I'm scared!' She stamped her trotter crossly. Aitor stood up and nuzzled her with his snout.

'Long ago, the hillside was very lonely because nothing would grow there. Every plant it asked refused, and the moors and hills became sadder and sadder. Finally word got around to one plucky little plant, who cheerfully volunteered to grow on the hillside. And ever since, that plant has not only grown on the moors, but has thrived there, making them more beautiful than anywhere else in the world. The name of that plant?'

'Heather?' said Heather, grumpily.

Aitor nodded. 'As a result, the name Heather has come to mean something, or someone, who is selfless and caring, someone who blossoms in the harshest places and lights up everything around them. Even in adversity. That means even when everything is against you.'

'I know what it means,' lied Heather, feeling a bit tearful. How did he always know the right thing to say? It was like he could see inside her and knew exactly what she was thinking. But Aitor couldn't see anything. He was completely blind. He didn't even know what she looked like. He was totally dependent on her to see everything. What was she doing being so pathetic? She must get up, pull herself together and lead them both out of here to safety. With new resolve, she stood up, cleared her throat and marched straight into the wall.

'Ouch.'

'It's this way. Just walk towards my voice.' Aitor was already a little way ahead.

'Wait!' squealed Heather. She very tentatively put one trotter forward, then another, then a third and finally the fourth. Phew. She started again, inching the first trotter forward, then the second —

'For heaven's sake! Can you speed up or we'll be here all day!'

'I'm going as fast as I can, but I can't see anything. It's difficult.'

Heather jumped as Aitor appeared next to her.

'Forget your eyes. Close them, and your other senses will become far more acute. Then use your nose. Pigs have incredible noses, but most of the time they only use them to find apples. Also, walk close to the wall, that way you can feel it and you know which way is forward.'

Annoyingly, he was right. The moment Heather closed her eyes, her sense of smell and her hearing became much better. She wasn't going to admit it, though, so she opened her eyes stubbornly.

'Better with your eyes shut?' asked Aitor.

'Er, yes,' squeaked Heather, her trotters firmly crossed. 'By the way,' she added quickly, 'how do you know we're headed the right way? Can you sense direction this far underground?'

'It's a tunnel, Eder, it only goes one way.'

Chapter 10

BATS!

Mr Hornbuckle eased through the door into the tunnel. It had taken him a long while to get out of the quarry, haul himself back up the hillside and prise the remaining planks away from the doorway. He was wet, battered, his clothes were torn; and he was quite grumpy. He'd had to leave Thomas outside. The dachshund hated small spaces and refused point blank to go into the mine. The pest controller had a light attached to a band on his head and it was showing him a steep tunnel, which seemed to lead towards a hole in the ground. He lay down next to the hole and peered into the darkness. The beam of his head-light was too weak to light all the way down but the pigs must be at the bottom. Probably dead, but he had to find out. He wrapped a rope around an overhead beam and started to lower himself down into the darkness.

He landed with a splash and shone his torch ahead to reveal the tunnel. The tunnel roof was supported by struts of wood on the ceiling every twenty or so metres. He was intrigued to see light bulbs hanging from a few of them as well. He looked around him until he found a control panel and a row of switches.

'Surely not . . . ?' he muttered under his breath as he experimentally flipped them all to *on*. After a delay of a few seconds, almost as if the bulbs were grumblingly waking up and moaning about who was disturbing them after all this time, they started to flicker into life and, at random points along the corridor, lights started to come on. Clearly visible in the light were the twin trotter tracks heading away down the tunnel. Horatio spotted them and cracked his knuckles gleefully.

Up ahead, Aitor and Heather were trotting onwards when the lights came on. Heather suddenly realised she could see where she was going and was pleased. That was better. Aitor stopped in his tracks, put his snout in the air and held it steady. Heather copied him, although she wasn't really sure what she was supposed to be sniffing.

'Can you feel that?' he asked excitedly.

'Yeah – um . . . what exactly?'

'That breeze. You can feel the air moving. It means there must be an exit somewhere ahead.'

Heather peered forwards.

'I can't see anything.'

'Of course you can't,' chuckled Aitor. 'It's too dark.'

Heather smiled with him. 'Not any more. The lights are on now.'

Aitor turned to her in horror. 'What? When did they come on?'

'Just now. Why?'

'Because if they weren't on when we started then it means there's someone down here. And they're only going to be down here for one thing. You.'

Heather gulped. He was right. She started to turn on the spot but Aitor stopped her.

'Listen.'

They both listened and, sure enough, further down the tunnel they could hear the very faint sound of footsteps.

'Oh oh oh. What do we do now?'

'We run.'

The tunnel was a bit lower here and Horatio felt something brush his head. He stopped for a second and cautiously shone his torch at the ceiling. What he'd thought was the roof was actually a carpet of bats – thousands of bats, all utterly motionless, and all hanging from the ceiling, asleep. There were so many of them, he felt almost like a trespasser. As if he'd strayed into someone else's house. He took a deep breath, crouched down and started to jog along the tunnel.

Heather and Aitor were running. Occasionally Aitor would stop to sniff at the air, before grimly hurrying on again. The breeze was stiffening and then they rounded a corner and Heather skidded to a halt, making Aitor bump into the back of her. Ahead of them, the tunnel split. One side was pretty much blocked with stones, the other stretched away into the distance. From behind them they could hear the chasing footsteps.

'What is it?' asked Aitor.

'The tunnel goes in two. One side is clear and the other's got loads of rocks.'

'Which side is the breeze coming from?'

Heather moved from side to side. 'It's weird. It's coming from the side that's completely blocked.'

'Then that's the way out. The other one must be a dead end. Tell me exactly what you see.'

'There's loads of things on the ceiling. They look like mice hanging by their tails.'

'Bats. The only mammals who fly. I like them because they don't use their eyes to see. They make noises, which travel and hit an object and then bounce back. Like an echo.'

'Yes, yes, very interesting. Can we get on? Anyway, they're not moving now,' said Heather.

'They're sleeping. We really don't want them to wake up.'

'Why not?'

'Never mind. What else?'

There were piles of different sized rocks stacked on top of each other, stretching from the floor of the tunnel right up to the roof. Then she described the tunnel to him – nearly two metres high with bits of wood on the sides.

'Sounds like some rocks have fallen and blocked the passage. Look for a gap. It must be there if air's coming through.'

'That will take hours. We haven't got time. He's coming.'

'Don't worry about him, just find that hole and make it bigger.'

Aitor disappeared back the way they'd come and Heather turned to face the solid wall of rock.

Mr Hornbuckle was moving fast along the tunnel now. It felt like it was getting narrower, though, and the lights were flickering on and off. He could feel a breeze, and that and the bats made him shiver. He pulled his coat around him before carrying on.

It was dark by the rock-fall and Heather could barely see. Was that a chink at the top? She scampered over to have a proper look. The rocks were slippery and it was hard work clambering up – she kept sliding back down and bruising her shins. Finally she found the little hole where the air was coming through. Now, if she could just move a few rocks out of the way, they might be able to squeeze through. She worked away and made a hole big enough for her shoulders. 'Aitor. Come now! I can make a hole. We can get through.'

She slid down the rock pile, raced around the corner and saw him running back and forth in the entrance to the other tunnel.

'What are you doing?'

'Tricking him. Can you get through yet?'

'I think so, come on.'

Then, to their horror, Mr Hornbuckle rounded the corner and saw them. He couldn't have been more than twenty metres away, so close Heather could see his curling moustache and the rips in his clothes from where he'd rolled all the way down the hill into the quarry.

For a second, time stood still as they stared at each other and then Mr Hornbuckle smiled, like the wildcat.

'Aitor!' yelped Heather. 'He's h-h-here! With his gun!'

'Squeal, Eder, as loud as you can!'

'But you said not to wake the bats!'

'Change of plan!' said Aitor and he started to roar.

Heather closed her eyes, took a deep breath and squealed as loud as she could. As Mr Hornbuckle raised his rifle and took aim, the noise from the two reached a crescendo and the bats woke up.

Furious at being roused from their sleep, and terrified by the noise of the pigs, the bats took off. Instantly it felt as if the tunnel had exploded inwards, as literally thousands and thousands of them dived, raced, swerved and whizzed all through the tunnel, pinballing everywhere like out-of-control black fireworks. There was something almost magical about the way they darted and weaved, never touching the walls and always pulling out of collisions with milliseconds to spare. But it was the noise that was truly terrifying. It was so loud that Heather couldn't hear, she couldn't see, she wanted to turn but she couldn't even do that.

Aitor came closer and shouted into Heather's ear. 'Quick, while they're distracting him, you need to go.'

'What do you mean?'

'You're going through that hole in the rocks, then you're going back to Scotland and you're going to get the farm back for Isla.'

'You are too!'

'No, Eder, not this time.'

'What! Why not?'

'Because it's the only way I can know you're safe. I will lead him the wrong way and give you time to escape.'

Heather shook her head. 'No!'

'Eder, you must trust me. I will lead him away and then I'll come and find you.'

Heather couldn't understand. She was getting more and more agitated. 'But why?'

'You've got to get the farm back for Isla. That's what matters.'

'No! Staying together is what matters!'

Aitor came closer and spoke firmly into her ear.

'Right now there are over seven hundred and fifty million pigs in the world. We live in every continent except Antarctica. No other animal has done this, and you know why? Because we're smart. We've watched humans, and we've learnt that when we work together, we achieve more. Which is why, Eder Duroc, you must dig yourself out of here, while I lead this man away. Got it?'

'But you said there was no way out of that tunnel. He'll catch you! He might even kill you!'

'Please, Eder, go! While there's still time!'

'I can't do it on my own! I'm scared!'

'It's good to be scared, it keeps you safe.'

Heather shook her head. 'No. I promised I wouldn't leave you and I won't. If you're going down that tunnel to be caught, then so am I.'

Aitor shook his massive head. He leant towards her and whispered in her ear again.

'But you're going to have piglets.'

Heather jumped like she'd been given an electric shock. 'How did you know? I only felt it myself a couple of days ago! I was going to tell you when we got to the farm.'

Aitor smiled sadly and touched her snout with his. 'I couldn't be certain, but you seemed so happy and, also, a bit . . . bigger?'

Heather smiled at him, but it was quite a wobbly smile.

Aitor nudged her towards the tunnel. 'Those piglets will be born free, Eder. That's why you have to go, for me and for them. Say hi to Isla . . . goodbye, my Eder . . .'

As the bats whirled around them, the two pigs had a last nuzzle, then they turned and ran their separate ways. Aitor disappeared down the tunnel as, choking with sobs, Heather scrambled up over the fallen rocks, rolled down the other side and ran blindly into the darkness. The two tunnels must have been side by side, because for a bit she could hear Aitor charging along, roaring so Mr Hornbuckle would follow him, sounding as if he was still by her side; but soon the tunnels must have moved apart because the sounds got fainter and fainter until Heather could hear nothing more and she gradually slowed to a walk and then stopped altogether.

Suddenly, for the first time since she'd found Isla in London all those months ago, Heather was all alone. The darkness closed in around her and she stood, an organically-raised, pure-breed Duroc pig, in a disused coal mine somewhere in the middle of England. Then the floodgates opened and she collapsed in a heap, wishing the world would end and take her with it.

Chapter 11

Angels and Ploughmen

Heather walked underground for what felt like days. Occasionally she would stop where she was and have a sleep and then get up when she woke and carry on. She had no idea where she was, or even if she was heading in the right direction. She had no food and not seeing the sun was starting to confuse and disorient her. It was only the thought of what Aitor had said to her that was keeping her going. He was right. She owed it to her piglets to get back to the surface.

She had left the mine tunnel behind her long ago. The excavations went deep into the hillside, but they were crisscrossed by the burrows, setts and warrens of the animals that lived underground, and that was the labyrinth that Heather found herself wandering through now. Finally, too weak to carry on, she collapsed and was asleep until an aggressive badger woke her and chased her up another tunnel. She saw a glimmer of light ahead and realised she was running uphill and, hopefully, finally reaching the surface.

Tired and hungry, Heather paused at the exit from the badger's sett and listened. The badger tried to shoo her out but she gave him a good kick and he grumbled back down into the tunnel, leaving her to investigate what was waiting for her outside the hole. She shut her eyes and heard a growing babble of voices, and as she sniffed, she got a confusing mixture of smells – lots of different humans, all sweaty and some of them quite grubby. It all reminded her of

Isla's smell, and that brought a huge lump to her throat. Where was her friend now? Then a voice started to speak so she stopped thinking and listened.

'Okay, Year Four, let's have a bit of hush. Can you all listen up, please? In a minute you can all eat your packed lunches and while we're doing that, Sophie is going to tell us a bit about the statue. Then you can all start your sketches and descriptions and remember – we're going to be using these as the basis for more classwork, so don't lose them! Right, gang, you're sick of the sound of my voice and you're all hungry so let's get on with lunch, but one more thing – can we please remember that there are other people around who want to enjoy being here, so I'd appreciate you keeping the noise down, and make sure you don't leave any rubbish behind when we go.'

Heather was suddenly overwhelmed as the smells from thirty lunchboxes drifted towards the sett where she was hiding, drenching her mouth with saliva and reminding her that she hadn't eaten for days. She was famished, and the more she thought about how hungry she was, the more her snout started acting on its own, pulling her further and further up the tunnel towards the tempting smells . . .

'Hey! Look here.' A boy's voice brought Heather back to her senses and as she slid quickly back inside the hole she saw shoes at the edge and then faces peering in. 'I'm sure I saw summat in there. What do you think it is? Fox? Rabbit? What?' Then, almost as if the gods were smiling on her, the boy took aim and threw an apple straight into the tunnel. It bounced and skidded around before rolling to a stop in front of the happy pig.

It was a Bloody Ploughman (*Scottish, deep red, with a crisp, sweet flavour*). As she bit into it, the farm came flooding back to her. She hadn't had one for as long as she could remember. Isla loved Ploughmen, and that made Heather realise something else. If there were Ploughmen in the lunchboxes, then she must be nearly home.

'Jack! James! Joseph!' came the loud voice of the teacher. 'Guys, can we show a little respect here please? Isabella, team point for you when we get back to school. Thank you. Right, gang, Sophie has given up her afternoon to come here with us, and I'd appreciate it if you could do her the courtesy of sitting down and listening to what she has to say. Do I make myself clear? Right. Sophie, over to you.'

Heather inched back up to the mouth of the sett and listened, as a voice like warm milk started to talk.

'Hello, boys and girls, my name's Sophie McKinlay and I'm here to tell you a little bit about the most amazing statue in Britain. Nelson's Column is also pretty impressive, but I think our Angel is up there with him. I'll give you some facts to begin with. The Angel is twenty metres high, which makes it taller than a five-storey building, and it has a wingspan of fifty-four metres, very nearly the same width as a jumbo jet.'

Heather couldn't resist it – she had to see what the woman was talking about, and very tentatively she poked her snout above ground and eased forward until she could see over the top of the hill. There was a class of children and a very young-looking teacher sitting there listening to the woman, but it was what was behind them that transfixed Heather. It looked like a vast man, impossibly tall, standing straight as a fence post with his legs together and stretching up into the sky, almost as high as she could see. But it wasn't just the body that was amazing, it was what stuck out from the sides. Where his arms should have been were two enormous wings, slightly tilted forward as though he was going to give you a massive hug, take off and fly up to the heavens, or stand guard for a thousand years. She had never seen anything so big and so powerful looking in all her life. But he wasn't frightening; actually, he was rather comforting. She couldn't exactly say why, but he made her feel safe.

'Miss? Why's it an angel?'

The class were all looking up at the statue as well and Heather wished Isla were there to see it. In her head, she started to describe it to Aitor, but she didn't have the words. This was something that needed to be seen.

'Good question. The artist – does anybody know the name of the artist who made it? No? His name is Antony Gormley. He's one of Britain's foremost living artists and builds lots of amazing things. Anyway, he said he had built an angel because nobody's ever seen one, but we need to keep imagining them. What do you think he meant by that?'

One of the girls put up her hand. 'It's like Megan was in the Christmas play. She didn't look anything like him, though. He's awesome.'

'Glad you like it. Personally, I've always felt that the artist meant that we all want something or someone who'll tell us what to do, who'll protect us when we're in danger and who'll forgive us when we mess up. Might be a mum, a friend, even a teacher. For Antony Gormley it was an angel. But, as it's seen by more than thirty-three million people every year, there's a lot of different opinions, and they're all right.'

Heather closed her eyes and listened as the children all said what they thought, did their drawings and then disappeared off, chatting excitedly about the statue as they went. She came out, had a good scavenge through the rubbish bin until she'd eaten her fill and then lay down at the foot of the Angel and thought about things. She'd been so busy walking underground that she hadn't had a think for a long time. As a result, there were lots of thoughts to be thought, so she lined them all up in a queue and told each one to be patient and that it would get its turn. She started off by wondering what had become of Aitor. Perhaps he was still somewhere in the darkness below her, leading Mr Hornbuckle a merry dance, and she felt glad that the Angel was up here watching over him. Then she thought about being pregnant and felt happy that she would have a living memory of Aitor, and she marvelled at how he'd known.

'*I didn't, Eder, it was just a guess.*'

She grinned to herself as she heard Aitor speaking in her head. Next it was Isla's turn. Heather got comfy and settled down to have a really good think about her best friend, stuck somewhere she didn't want to be, but making the best of it as she always did. She wondered what she was doing at the moment, whether she was still being looked after by that funny woman who sounded like her words were coming out backwards when she spoke. That was a really nice thought, but the next one in the queue was a scary, big one. It was more of a memory, really, a reminder that she'd promised to get the farm back for Isla and make everything back to how it used to be. That was way too big to think about so she shook her head and pushed it to the back of the queue. Then she moved on to thinking about food. But even that couldn't keep her awake and, right in the middle of remembering a delicious leek she'd once found in Isla's vegetable patch, she fell fast asleep.

When she woke up she felt much better. She had a lot to do, and no idea how to do it but, somehow, looking up at the Angel, it didn't seem so bad. Somehow she knew it would all be okay. The Angel had guided her out of the coal mine, and now would stand guard over Aitor, and keep an eye on her as she carried on with her long walk home. She looked at the sun, high up in the sky, positioned herself so it was shining down on her right flank, and started walking.

To: Millie Raphael-Campbell
From: Isla Wolstenholme

I'm in the car on the motorway! Dad's phone can send emails from anywhere so right now we've just driven past this amazing statue of a huge angel just outside Newcastle. We stopped and had lunch by it. So Cool. I thought it was wicked, but Dad reckons it looks like a clothes peg! We've got a lift with Nikki who's the really nice woman who used to look after Heather and she's going to get the new Busby to go to our farm for the school visit you told me about! So exciting! Can't wait to see you.

Love Isla

xxxxxxxx

PS Dad's got this computer game called Farmland and you have to be a pretend farmer with sheep and chickens and cows. It's quite cool but not very real because the hens lay eggs every five minutes and the cows get really fat until you milk them. Ask your dad if you can get it and then we can meet in the game.

To: Isla Wolstenholme
From: Millie Raphael-Campbell

That's wicked. Just downloaded the game – it's not my birthday for ages so I had to ask Dad for like three weeks of early pocket money. My farm's called Millie's Milkhouse. What's yours called? I have to play it on my dad's computer which is really old so it takes like an hour to shear the sheep. Bad news. My manky brother has got chicken pox. Mum says she'll fix you somewhere else to stay if you've never had it!
Love Millie
xxxxxxxxxxx
PS Miss Stephenson wants you to come and do a show and tell about London!

Chapter 12

Home Is Where the Sword Is

Heather wasn't sure how long it took her to get from the Angel to the farm but it felt like she'd been walking all her life. Her trotters ached, but the squashy heather underneath was cool and comforting. Every day she got more used to finding her own way as she followed Aitor's instructions; looking at the sun during the day, and then using the stars at night to point her in the right direction. She ate whatever she could find – berries and other fruit, wild mushrooms growing in the damp earth underneath trees and, on one occasion, she even found a funny, knobbly thing buried under the ground by a tree. It had an amazing smell and she couldn't help rooting and rooting until she'd dug it out and then gobbled it up. It was delicious.

'It's a truffle, Eder. Humans love them and charge lots of money for them. They use pigs to hunt for them because we have such excellent noses, we can find them easily.'

She jumped and looked around for Aitor. Obviously he wasn't there, but that had definitely been his voice in her head. He'd told her about truffles ages ago! How funny that that memory should come back now, and in his voice! Funny, but nice, almost as if he was still walking next to her, the two of them chatting away happily. Maybe that's what Isla felt about her mum?

Heather was singing a lot as well. Aitor had always encouraged what he called 'marching songs', so you walked to the rhythm of the song and sort of forgot how much you were walking because you were too busy singing. Unfortunately Heather was a bit forgetful, so she could only remember one. It was sung to the tune of 'Happy Birthday'.

'And the pigs will march on,
And the pigs will march on.
Eating acorns and apples,
Keeps us healthy and strong!'

It had been such a long journey, but now she was finally here, sitting at the top of the hill dividing her farm from Mr McDonald's sheep farm next door. She felt so different, she'd seen so many things, travelled so far; and yet, here she was, back again in the one place in the world where she felt completely comfortable. It was like nowhere else, and until now she hadn't realised how much she missed it, and how desperate she had been to get home.

'Look, Aitor. Down there. That's Farmer McDonald's sheep farm. Can you see the dog herding the sheep into the pen? It's not Blackie, though, he must have got a new dog. I suppose lots of things will have changed.'

'*Bit thoughtful, Eder?*'

'I suppose I am,' said Heather, feeling rather grown up at having important things to think about.

Aitor chuckled. '*You look ridiculous. Thinking doesn't suit you.*'

'Oi! Can I just remind you you're only alive in my head, thank you very much. I can switch you off whenever I want.'

Heather looked down at her farmyard. She was a bit alarmed to see enormous fences ringing the whole farm.

'Those fences are new, though. They're huge. How am I going to get in? Perhaps I should wait for Alastair to come out for a run? Then he can tell everyone I'm here? That's best. I'll have a little snooze while I wait.'

'*That's your plan? To have a snooze and do nothing?*' Aitor snorted in her head. Heather shushed him and lay down.

But somehow she just couldn't get comfy, something was niggling her. She didn't know what, but she was definitely feeling a sort of pull towards something on the other side of the hill. She got up and waggled a trotter, which was the one bit of her that had gone to sleep, and then set off. There was a spring bubbling out of the rocks at the top of the next hill and she drank deeply, the water cool and crisp on her snout.

When she realised where she was, she scampered happily down the hill. At the bottom was the ruined castle, Isla's favourite spot in the world.

'Look, Aitor, this is the place I told you about. That's the ruined castle and that's where Isla's mum's buried. Her vegetables are a tiny bit overgrown, but actually it's quite tidy, and the tree's still good. Did I tell you about the ghost tree? It looks dead but it's not. That's what Isla says. She says it's all because there was this boy who accidentally betrayed his dad when he was hiding from the soldiers. The soldiers killed his dad and Isla said the son feels guilty, like it was his fault his father died and that's why the tree has no fruit. Because he's hunting it.'

'*I think you mean* haunting *the tree, Eder, but you're right – I can feel the history here too.*'

Heather looked up at the tree, standing proud and strong, centuries old and still stubbornly refusing to bear any fruit. She remembered it waving to her all those months ago and now she smiled at it fondly.

'Hello, tree, I'm back.'

That was weird. There was an apple growing on the tree. Just one. The rest of it looked as dead as ever – no leaves, nothing. But there was one solitary apple, hanging invitingly. Her stomach rumbled thoughtfully. It wasn't like any apple she'd ever seen before and, in fact, hadn't Isla's dad said it *wasn't* an apple tree? What was it? A muddler? A middler? Something like that. Either way, there was one delicious looking fruit dangling juicily just out of reach. She wanted it. She stood up on her hind legs, leaned against the tree and tried to reach it. No good. It was too far back. She reached further and further, tilting back and back until . . . *thump*. Over she went. Bother.

It was no good, she was going to have to jump. She stood underneath the fruit, bent her legs and leapt. Then she leapt again. And again. Still not high enough. Heather walked a little way off and looked at it. Then, thinking she'd take it by surprise, she ran, bent her legs and jumped. This time she brushed the fruit with her snout before landing again. She tutted and tried again.

After about half an hour of jumping, she still hadn't got it.

'Good jumping, Auntie Heather,' said Thom.

'All that walking's made your legs strong,' added Ramelan.

Heather looked round in surprise but there was no one there. She grinned. She was used to having Aitor in her head, but she hadn't had the twins before.

'Hey, look. What's that?' asked Ramelan.

'What?' Heather asked herself (after all, he was inside her head so really she was talking to herself).

'That! The thing in the ground,' replied Thom.

Heather looked. Her vigorous jumping had actually scooped away the earth under the tree and made a hole. Not a big hole, but certainly a dip in the ground, and inside the dip was something shiny. Perhaps it was another one of those delicious truffles? She started to snuffle around the thing at the bottom of the tree. The earth was lovely and particularly good for rooting; it was sort of chocolatey – all dark, rich and moist – and so cool on her bruised and battered snout.

As she rooted and cleared the earth, she started to get the strangest feeling. A feeling of inevitability, as though she was meant to be here, as though the fruit on the tree had got her jumping for a reason, almost as if it wasn't her who was trying to get hold of something, but the other way round…

Fairly soon her snout had cleared a space around the thing and she stepped back to examine it. What she saw was a sort of metal basket with a handle inside it. She cleared away some more earth and found that whatever it was that she'd uncovered was actually stuck inside the roots of the tree. It may once have been placed under them, but over the years the roots had grown around it and over it and through it, until now it was not just hidden under the tree, it was part of it.

That wasn't going to deter Heather. The mystery fruit had made her find this thing, so now she was going to have it. She bent down, gripped it between her teeth and gave a little exploratory tug. It didn't even budge. Bother. She tried again, but no luck. It was stuck fast. Aitor came to her rescue.

'Try pushing instead of pulling. See if you can loosen it that way.'

Sure enough, that did seem to work a bit. Now she could jiggle it better. She gripped the handle in her mouth and started to wiggle it properly. It was getting looser, still stiff, but it was starting to come. She stretched backwards and heaved. Slowly and grudgingly, the thing started to come out of the tree. It was like those hankies the magician had pulled out of Isla's ear at her birthday party, only more solid. Suddenly, like a cork out of a bottle, it shot out of the roots of the tree, sending Heather flying onto her back and making her open her mouth and let go of the handle. The thing flew through the air, turning and glinting as the sunlight caught it, before landing point down in the ground where it stuck, quivering gently and swaying, like a really tall, shiny, metal flower.

'It's a sword,' said Thom, sounding awestruck.

Ramelan was equally impressed. *'It must have been there for years.'*

Heather peered into the hole left by the sword and saw a canvas bag at the bottom. She picked it up in her mouth and the old, rotten cloth ripped open and shiny gold coins poured out and lay in a big heap at the bottom of the hole, glinting at her chirpily. Heather peered at them closely. There was something very familiar about them, but she couldn't think what.

Anyway, the sword was quite pretty and she was sure Isla would like it, so she put it into the hole at the bottom of the tree, covered the lot with earth and then sat on top of it all like a rather large red chicken on a nest of golden eggs.

The fruit was still hanging from the tree and she looked at it longingly as her tummy rumbled. Suddenly, as she stared, and almost as if it had done its job and could now relax, it fell off the tree, bounced once and landed smack bang in front of Heather. It was sort of open at one end, a bit like an animal's bottom, she thought to herself and then blushed at being rude. She opened her mouth and —

'Heather!'

That voice wasn't in her head! She turned round and, there, jumping up and down on the other side of the fence, were her two best four-legged friends! Alastair the sheepdog and Rhona the goat.

Chapter 13

Foe
or Friend?

'What are you doing here?' cried all three animals at once.

'We come and look after the garden for Isla.'

'I've come to get the farm back for Isla.'

It had been so long since Heather had seen Alastair and Rhona that they all started talking at once, and then they stopped and then started again until finally Rhona raised a hoof and shushed them. She and Alastair were desperate to hear about her adventures, so Heather gave them a short version of everything that had happened. Then it was their turn.

Alastair went first. 'Someone called Mr Hornbuckle turned up two weeks ago and is camped out in one of the fields, waiting for you. He says he's been chasing you for months but you keep escaping. Nobody believes him but he's sure you're coming back here and he's determined to catch you when you do. The pest control agency sacked him when he told them that you'd escaped from an underground mine. I know that because I sat outside his tent last week and listened to him talking to his dog. Anyway, Mr Busby has said he can stay until after the big presentation but then he's got to go. He spends all day looking for any signs of you. He's determined to show everyone that he's not mad.'

Heather was a bit gloomy that Mr Hornbuckle was still around; after all, it was his fault she wasn't introducing them to Aitor, but she put that to one side.

'What's happened to Blackie? I saw a new dog herding Mr McDonald's sheep today. He was much better.'

Alastair blushed, but Heather could see he was really pleased.

'That was me. Blackie cut his paw on some barbed wire so I've been helping. It's okay – I mean, it's no big deal, I don't mind helping out, you know, when he really needs me.'

Behind him Heather could see Rhona rolling her eyes and guessed that Alastair might not be being completely honest about how excited he was.

Then Rhona took over. 'And there's all this stuff happening with Busby. All the schools are doing a healthy eating thing and they're coming to see round the factory. The new Busby pig is going to be there so Mr Busby's got photographers coming and everything. It's all happening the day after tomorrow.'

But Rhona had saved the best bit of news for last. 'Isla's here.'

'No!' Heather jumped up and started turning round and round with sheer excitement.

'Yes! Turns out Nikki, who looked after you, is looking after the new Busby as well and she's good friends with Isla and Farmer Wolstenholme so they've come along with her.'

Alastair was looking a bit sheepish and Heather grinned as she remembered something. 'Has she brought her dog Izzy with her?'

Rhona nodded.

'Does she still say "yup" all the time?'

'Only when Alastair asks her something,' teased Rhona.

'We're just friends!' protested Alastair but Heather could see he was embarrassed and she snorted happily. She was very fond of Izzy and still remembered how the little celebrity-obsessed dog had helped her escape in the middle of London.

'Why is Isla staying here? It can't just be so Alastair can flirt with Izzy.'

Rhona grinned. 'Isla's friend's got chicken pox so Nikki asked Mr Busby if they could stay in the farmhouse. Isla would be so excited if she knew you were here.'

Knowing that her best friend was so close made Heather even more determined to get inside the farm. She must find a way.

'Any ideas on how I can get in?' she asked her two friends.

Rhona shook her head grimly. 'It's impossible. These are electric fences. If we touch them we get a really bad shock. A friend of Alastair's tried it to see what would happen and he limped for a whole week.'

Alastair nodded. 'You could pretend to be Busby. I mean, you are Busby, but you could pretend to be the one who's really pretending to be you and really you'd be being the real Busby but everyone'd think you were the fake.'

'Doesn't get me inside, though,' said Heather reasonably.

They all thought for a minute.

'What about if I just come straight through the front gate?'

'There are CCTV cameras, especially now with

the presentation coming up. It can't be done.'

'What about the wildcat?' asked Heather. 'Does he still get in?'

Rhona nodded. 'What do you think all the security's for? There are snares and traps everywhere, and Mr Busby's even poisoned the rabbits. Hasn't worked, though. The wildcat still comes in. I think he does it just to prove he can.'

'He's only feeding his family,' said Heather. 'No different to the rest of us.'

Rhona looked at her friend thoughtfully. She seemed different. Almost...wiser. Rhona grinned at the thought, as Heather stood up.

'Where does he live?' Heather asked.

'By the river, I think. Why?'

'I'm going to find him and ask him how he does it.'

Alastair looked at Heather as if she was totally mad. 'I'm coming with you.'

Heather shook her head. 'He'll smell you. I have to go alone.'

'What if you don't come back?'

'I will.'

They chatted for a while longer and then the other two went back to the farm for tea. Heather had a doze and then set out. She walked all the way to the river that ran through the forest and started to have a good look around.

'*Eder, go into the forest. Maybe wildcats like living among the trees.*' Aitor was inside her head again.

She checked out a couple of holes, but they were old and uninhabited, and then she saw a badger slinking into a hole under a large tree.

'*They are also very lazy —*'

'So he might just use a badger's sett,' interrupted Heather.

She was about to approach for a closer look when a gust of wind blew over the hole towards her and she got a snout-full of that musky, unmistakably wildcatty smell. It was so distinctive and so familiar that Heather nearly turned tail and fled. Smell can conjure up memories of places, people, and even how you felt the last time you smelt that particular smell. For Heather, that musky smell of wildcat took her right back to the farmyard. Back to one particular time, a memory of an utterly terrifying moment when she'd been trying to protect the chickens and the wildcat had bared his teeth, licked his lips, stuck his muzzle right into her snout and said —

'Hello, Fatty . . .'

The whispered voice came from above Heather and she squealed, ran, and then frantically looked upwards. The wildcat was lounging on a branch two metres up in the air and, as she watched, he dropped soundlessly to the ground and sat there, his tail gently flicking, looking cruel, a little bit amused, and very, very frightening. He smiled hungrily.

'You've lost weight. How . . . disappointing.'

Heather had her back to a tree now as she tried to gather her thoughts, but she'd been so muddled by being caught unawares, that she forgot the speech she'd carefully planned and just blurted, 'Help!'

The wildcat cocked his head sideways. 'I don't think anyone can hear you. Although that was a very loud squeal.'

'No, I . . . I mean, I . . . I need your help.'

'Indeed? Is this the last request of a condemned

pig?' He yawned, his teeth sharp and saw-like.

'You can get inside the farm. I need to know how you do it.'

'And why should I tell you?'

Heather picked up a dead rabbit she'd got Alastair to find for her earlier and dropped it in front of the wildcat.

'A gift? That's very nice, but I think I might prefer a nice leg of pork.'

'Look at it.'

The wildcat looked down at the rabbit and recoiled, pulling his lips back over his teeth with a hiss of disgust. Heather moved a step closer.

'He did this. The new farmer. He hates you and he's poisoned the rabbits so that they'll die out and you'll have nothing left to eat.'

At that moment, two young wildcat cubs exploded out of the burrow, rolling around and play fighting. They rolled and rolled and then they saw their dad, sitting still and staring at them. Instantly they sat up straight and tucked their tails in behind them.

But the strangest thing of all was that they'd been

playing in complete silence. The wildcat looked at them.

'Go in to your mother, tell her I'll be there shortly.' He threw them a pair of dead field mice.

The cubs grabbed the mice and disappeared back down the burrow. Heather was curious.

'Why are they so quiet? Are they scared?'

The wildcat snarled. 'When successful hunting depends on surprise, it's as well to learn the value of silence.'

'But they were playing.'

'*Especially* when they're playing.'

At that point one of the kittens stuck his head out of the hole. 'Sir? Mama says will your friend be staying for dinner?'

The wildcat smiled. 'My friend *is* the dinner. Or she will be. Soon.'

The kitten looked confused and disappeared back down the hole.

Heather was a mixture of scared and appalled. '*Sir?* Your children call you sir?'

'They respect me. When you respect someone you

address them respectfully . . . Fatty.'

Heather raised her snout crossly but chose to ignore the insult. The wildcat was still looking thoughtful.

'I'll just kill more chickens.'

'But how long will it be until he catches you? Dogs, the electric fence, men with guns, and now he's put traps in the rabbit holes. What next?'

She saw the wildcat react. He obviously hadn't known about the traps. He snarled at her. 'And? What do you suggest?'

'I can get him to leave. Get the old farmer back. He'll pull the fences down and the rabbits will recover. Then you can eat them as much as you want.'

The wildcat looked interested, if a bit dubious. 'How are you going to do that?'

'That's not your concern. Just get me into the farm and I'll do the rest.'

The wildcat looked amused. 'You seem different, Fatty. More . . . determined? I hope all this new backbone hasn't spoilt your flavour. I'll make you a deal. You've got a week to do what you promised or you come back here and . . . well, let's just say even with all the weight you've lost, I don't think my family would go hungry for a while.'

'Just tell me.' Heather quavered.

The wildcat licked his lips. 'You're best off going in at night. There's a long, underground tunnel which leads from just by the stile to the wall of the cellar where he keeps the other chickens. There are some loose bricks there you can remove. It's all sealed off, but you can get up the conveyor belt into the factory from there. You'll see the machines that chop up the chickens before they get put into packets. Up on one side is an air duct. You have to climb up to reach it but it opens out onto the farmyard. There's a roof below you can jump onto.'

'What do you mean, the other chickens?'

'The ones that live in the cellar underneath the factory. The real "Busby Birds". You didn't think he actually sells the ones that run about in the open air? They're just for show. And for me, of course.'

Heather was confused. 'But why?'

'Because it's how he makes his money. Everybody wants free-range chickens that have been bred in the open air, but it's expensive to keep them like that, and Busby is greedy. So he cheats. He can raise many more in the cellar, pass them off as free range, and nobody will ever know.'

'But that's wrong. Why haven't you done anything?'

The wildcat laughed. 'I have the perfect way into the farm – why would I do anything?'

'But I don't understand. If there's loads of chickens in the cellar, why don't you just eat them?'

The wildcat shuddered. 'They are disgusting. I would never eat them, let alone feed them to my cubs. They are kept in a barn all their lives so they grow fat, but their legs can't support their weight and they can't move around so they develop no muscles and don't taste of anything. It's so cramped they are given pills to keep them free of disease, other pills to make them fat, they live less than six weeks, and for those six weeks the lights are on twenty-four hours a day so they never sleep, which makes them eat even more. Thanks, but I think I'll stick to the ones that run about in the fresh air.'

As the wildcat disappeared into his earth, Heather

looked at the sky and realised it was nearly time to meet her friends again. She still had absolutely no idea how she was going to do what she'd now promised the wildcat, as well as Aitor, but getting the farm back could wait until tomorrow. She felt a warm glow start in her tummy and spread all over her. An Isla-glow. Tonight she was going to see Isla.

Chapter 14

The Underworld

Mr Hornbuckle sat bolt upright and looked at his watch. It read two minutes past midnight, and he was puzzled. Why had he woken up? Something had disturbed him. Something . . . something . . . something piggish. He unzipped his sleeping bag and extracted his long legs. His tent was far too small and he was much too big, so from the outside, whenever he tried to move or do anything, bits of him pushed against the side of the tent, making weird shapes and angles like someone trying to get a coat hanger through a shirt.

Once he was dressed he stepped outside and looked up at the sky. The moon was bright and full, a 'bomber's moon', so called because it allowed wartime pilots on night missions to see their targets clearly. Sadly, as in the case of his own grandfather, it also allowed the gunners on the ground a clear sight of the slow, lumbering planes, an irony which had meant his grandfather spent much of the Second World War in a prisoner-of-war camp in Germany, having been shot down on a night-time bombing run over Hamburg.

By the time Horatio knew him, his grandfather was in his seventies and would never talk about the war, but Horatio's abiding memory of him was of a man who had obviously hated being locked up – so much so, that even thirty years later, he could still never spend more than about six hours inside his house at any one time. Horatio would quite often find him outside, regardless of whether it was day or night, gazing out across the open fields, or pretending to oil the garden gate just so he could walk through it over and over again. Horatio would ask him what he was doing and the old man wouldn't really know. He'd laugh and say he was just being silly, but Horatio didn't believe him. There was more to it than that. He could still remember how angry his grandfather had become when he discovered that Horatio had locked his sister in the loo and was laughing at her through the door. His grandfather couldn't explain it, but Horatio was left with a clear sense of how being locked up, against your will, can be a terrifying, cruel thing.

Things had been difficult since he had been sacked by the pest control company. They said he'd gone mad – but he knew better. He was sure that that pig was still alive, and also that sooner or later she'd turn up here. It was just a matter of when. Could it be this evening? Something had made him wake up, and following his instincts had never let him down before. He ducked back into his tent, collected his net and set off. Time to go hunting.

Heather was underground again. She was following the wildcat's directions and trotting through a tunnel towards the cellar under the factory.

When she reached the wall, she discovered that the cement had fallen out and, as the wildcat had said, it was actually quite easy to push away the bricks and make a small entrance. When she did, not only did light flood out into her little tunnel, but she was also thumped in the snout by the nastiest smell she'd ever smelt. She told herself to be brave, took a deep breath, squeezed in her stomach and half rolled, half slid through to the other side. What she saw when she got up would stay with her for ever.

Mr Hornbuckle had climbed over the gate and was now in the farmyard. He sniffed but smelt nothing unusual; he shut his eyes and listened, but there were no unusual sounds. He was just thinking that perhaps his hunch had led him astray when he spotted something that made him duck back into the shadows and stay very still. Over by the tool shed were the dog and the goat, sitting very still. This was most interesting. As he watched, the dog cocked his ears and looked up. Mr Hornbuckle followed his eyeline and saw that the dog was looking up at a hole in the wall that was surely the end of an air vent. Very quietly, he lowered himself to the ground and got comfortable.

Heather found herself in a room the size of a football pitch, with lights blazing and three fans hanging down, blowing air around the vast, cavernous space. But it wasn't the size of the room that was upsetting Heather, it was what it contained. Chickens. Hundreds of them. Tens of hundreds, even. Everywhere she looked there were chickens, crammed together, standing up, lying down, some on top of the others, some moving aimlessly in circles, some completely still. Some looked like they actually couldn't move, they were so squashed. The one thing they all had in common was a glazed, grey, dead look in their eyes.

Everywhere she looked was a solid yellow and white carpet of fat, young chickens – but not healthily young, or nicely fat. These were animals that had been forced fat, animals that had been fed so much food, and so many drugs, and kept in the light for so long, that they were too heavy for their own legs to support them. It was just as the wildcat had described it. These chickens literally couldn't stay upright.

And then there was the smell. Fresh chicken poo, old chicken poo, dead chickens, rotting chickens and old food. Heather choked again, her tummy coming up into her throat, and she slid back into the tunnel where she was violently sick.

'Where is she? She said midnight, and it's well past that,' muttered Alastair, looking up at the clock.

'She'll be here, don't worry. Anyway, that clock chimed forty-three times once – I wouldn't rely on it,' replied Rhona, trying hard not to show how worried she was.

Heather was back inside the chicken house. Now she was prepared for the smell, it wasn't quite such a shock and she was able to take it in better. The problem was that she could very clearly see the way out, but it was right over on the other side. How was she actually going to get across the room? She started sliding her feet forward, trying to push the chicks to one side and get past, but there were so many and they were packed so tight that getting through was going to be a painfully slow business.

Horatio stretched his legs out. The dog and the goat still hadn't moved; they were definitely up to something. He looked at his watch. It was one o'clock in the morning. He'd give it five more minutes.

Heather finally reached the other side of the room. There was a sort of ramp there which led up into a machine and that seemed the most sensible way out so she jumped onto it. It was like a belt on rollers which must be used to take the chickens up into the factory on the floor above. It was also a bit like the escalators in the Tube, but this one wasn't moving. From her vantage point, she looked back at the sea of chickens and shuddered. They almost didn't seem to have noticed that a pig had just crossed the room.

She bent down and spoke to the nearest one. 'Excuse me?'

The chicken turned to look at her with glazed, empty eyes. 'Yes?'

Heather didn't know what to say. 'When was the last time you were outside?'

'Outside?'

'Outside. You know, in the farmyard. Where the sun is.'

'I live in here.'

The chicken turned away and tried to move but didn't have the room or the energy so just stayed where she was. Heather didn't know what to do, she was just so . . . so . . . so . . . angry. This was no way to treat any creature, even one that was only being bred to be eaten. She wasn't stupid. She understood that a lot of animals were only raised to provide meat for humans. A lot of her piglets got sold and turned into food, but at least they had a good life before they were taken away. But this? This was horrible. If this was how Mr Busby treated chickens, then he should be stopped. She didn't know how, but this couldn't be allowed.

How was it Aitor had described the Underworld? A place of pain and suffering, with no light or hope. That was where she was, right now. She cleared her throat and shouted out across the barn. 'I've got to go now, but I'm going to come back for you. I don't know how, but I'm going to get you all out of here. Just make sure you don't eat any pomegranate seeds!'

Chapter 15

The Boot and the Wrong Foot . . .

Isla sat bolt upright and shivered. Her dad was fast asleep in his bed across the room. The curtains were blowing in the breeze and she went over to the window and peered out. There was an amazing full moon – everything was bathed in a cold, silvery light, and the farmyard looked exactly as she remembered it. She couldn't say anything about this to her dad, but she almost wished they hadn't come back. It had felt so natural arriving and seeing Alastair and Rhona, but then Mr Busby had appeared and now he was sleeping in her old room and she and her dad were in the spare room, and all in all she felt like a guest in her own house.

Where was Heather? Somehow she'd been so sure that her friend would have found her way back here and be waiting for her. Her dad had told her to try not to live in the past so much, and she knew he was right. Coming back was good because it made her realise that she would always love it here, but it had changed.

She wasn't going to be sad in London any more, there was no point. She leant her head against the cold glass of the window and, just for a moment, allowed herself to really think about Heather and wonder if she'd ever see her again. She'd been so sure – almost as if the farm was so magic it would pull them all here like a magnet. But it hadn't. She leant forward to close the window and the coin on the string around her neck swung forward. She held it tightly in her hand and smiled as she remembered

Heather finding it in the field and giving it to her, and then she herself giving it back to Heather when she left the farm, before it was finally returned to her at London Zoo. It glinted at her, twinkling as the moonlight reflected off its shiny surface. Isla smiled sadly. Perhaps she'd find her friend, and perhaps not. Either way it was time for a fresh start. She twirled the coin on its string and went back to bed.

Heather was inside the factory. This floor was the same size as the one below but it couldn't have been more different. A vast array of machinery just waiting for the chickens so it could get on with its gruesome job of chopping, cleaning and packaging. It seemed impossible that this used to be the barn where she'd been born and spent so many years of her life. It was unrecognisable now, all full of machines and plastic things. She hadn't been in here since the fire – it seemed a lifetime ago. She shivered at the memory and looked around until she found the air vent the wildcat had mentioned. It was a bit high, but she'd come this far. Determinedly, she started to climb.

Alastair was pacing up and down. 'What if she's been caught? We've heard nothing.'

'Which means she can't have been caught. It must just be more difficult to get out than she thought. Will you stand still?'

'I'm going to do another circuit, see if I can see anything.'

'Shh! I can hear something.'

They both looked up at the air vent and listened intently. Then, with a sound a bit like a large pig squeezing herself through a small air vent, Heather's head emerged. She looked slightly out of breath, quite squished and very serious.

Mr Hornbuckle was staring, open-mouthed. It was extraordinary. Busby, the pig he thought had died a hundred times and who had avoided capture many more, was coming out of an air vent! Now was his chance. She'd have to come down off that roof. He dropped to a crouch and started to move through the shadows.

'Ooof!' Heather grunted and wheezed as she squeezed through the vent.

Mr Hornbuckle was in position. He couldn't see the air vent now but he was waiting underneath the roof. He'd found a sheet, laid it on the ground and gathered the ends up so he could easily snare the pig the moment she landed. There were scamperings on the roof above and then a noise which reminded him of the way his grandfather used to put one finger inside his mouth and then pull it out with a huge pop. He braced himself. Any second now . . . yes! She flew through the air and landed slap in the middle of the sheet. He closed it around the struggling, writhing animal, grabbed the bundle in both arms and sprinted through the gate. He reached his car and put the squirming pig in the boot. Then he jumped into the front seat and turned the engine on. It roared triumphantly and he smiled as he headed out of the farm.

Mr Hornbuckle pulled in at the all-night garage in

Tullynessle to fill the car up with petrol. Angus, the boy who did the night shift, was a bit surprised to get any customers at this time of night, let alone one who was so chirpy and bouncy. Mr Hornbuckle insisted on buying a Twix 'to celebrate' and then bought Angus one as well. He paid and, happily munching, he headed back to the car, where he paused to look contentedly at the pig-full boot.

'Angus!' he called out.

The boy in the petrol station was a bit suspicious of this strange man who'd demanded to know his name and bought him chocolate, but he stuck his head out of the garage anyway. 'Wha'?'

'Have a guess what I've got in the boot of this car. You never will.'

Angus quite liked these games. 'Three hundred weight of potatoes?'

'Nope.'

'A collapsible helicopter?'

'Wrong again.'

The boy screwed up his face and thought really hard. 'Snow!'

Mr Hornbuckle smiled and shook his head.

'I'll tell you. It's a very well-known pig that I've been chasing for close to a year now and, this evening, I finally caught her.'

'Oh aye. That'll be Busby. Or Haither, as we used tae call her.'

'Indeed, indeed. I'll show you, but we'd better be careful, she's quite jumpy.'

He slowly opened the boot. The bundle was lying still, depressed and beaten. Carefully, proudly and respectfully, he unrolled the sheet to reveal . . .

. . . the sheepdog?

Angus was standing next to him. 'Tha's nae a pig. Tha's Alastair, Mr Busby's dog. 'Lo, Alastair, will ye hae some Twix?'

And as realisation dawned on Mr Hornbuckle that he'd been hoodwinked once more, Alastair barked cheerfully at Angus and then happily munched away at half of the lad's celebration chocolate before leaping out of the boot of the car and running back towards the farm.

While this was going on, Heather and Rhona were

sneaking around the side of the farmhouse. They'd waited until Mr Hornbuckle was safely gone before climbing down from the roof together. They were so lucky that Rhona had seen Heather in trouble and she and Alastair had gone up to help her. Alastair had spotted Mr Hornbuckle hiding and had volunteered to spring the trap.

Rhona was briefing Heather now. 'Everything's moved around. Mr Busby is in Isla's old bedroom and she's in the downstairs guest room. I checked it out earlier and the window was open so you should be able to wriggle in.'

They reached the farmhouse, manoeuvred some logs over, and Heather scrambled up and nudged the window open.

She could see Isla's toe poking out from under the duvet so she trotted mischievously over and gently nibbled it. It didn't taste like Isla's toe at all, and then, in a heart-stopping moment, a man's voice from under the duvet said very clearly, 'Chicken, please.' She was in the wrong room!

Heather was frozen. She couldn't move as Mr

Busby himself, dressed in green and red pyjamas, sat bolt upright like a rake that's been trodden on, rubbed his eyes, grunted, put on his spectacles and then saw the frozen Heather and howled 'AAAAAH!' at the top of his terrified voice.

Lights went on all over the farmhouse. Mr Wolstenholme came running in with Isla and then Nikki arrived with the other pig. By then Heather's legs had unfrozen and she'd jumped onto the table and scrambled out the bedroom window. As Mr Busby babbled about pigs and everyone grumbled sleepily, only Isla saw the muddy trotter prints on the table by the window. She went over and her heart did a triple somersault as she saw a tuft of red hair, caught in the window frame.

'Heather. You *are* here!'

Chapter 16

'Don't Be
a Chicken . . .'

The school bus pulled into the farmyard and the doors opened, letting hundreds of primary school children pour off, just like at the beach when your sandcastle wall gives way and the water runs out all over the place. As their teachers tried to group them into lines and restore some order, Isla spotted her class from Old Meldrum Primary and raced over to say hi.

'Millie! Hi!'

'Isla, hi!'

Everyone was there and they all clustered around Isla, asking questions and chattering away like they'd only seen her yesterday. Iain, Jimmy, Kirsty, Tullynessle Morag, Raj – everyone seemed to have stuff to say to her and she realised how much missed them all.

'Where's Miss Stephenson? I should tell her I'm here.'

'She's poorly so we've got a supply. He's called Mr Le Four and he's Canadian,' said Iain.

Isla introduced herself to Mr Le Four who was really tall and seemed very pleased to see her.

'Miss Stephenson told me you might well be tagging along with the class. She said you might have a friend with you, too. Heather, was it?'

The teacher obviously had no idea Heather was a pig, and Isla grinned.

'She's here somewhere – I'll introduce you later.'

As Mr Le Four tried to get everyone to stand still so he could count them, Isla turned to Millie.

'She is here!' she whispered. 'Last night she tried to

come into my bedroom but she went into his by accident!' She pointed at Mr Busby as she spoke.

He was standing on a sort of stage just in front of the barn, checking the microphone was working and looking slightly scared. Nikki stood next to him, holding the new Busby pig on a lead. At that point, Mr Le Four called them all together and they were taken into the factory to be shown round.

Millie clapped her hand over her mouth. 'No way! That's so cool. Did you see her?'

'No. He screamed really loudly and that woke us all up but by the time we ran into his room she must have got spooked and run off! I've been looking for her since I got up but I can't find her. Keep your eyes peeled!'

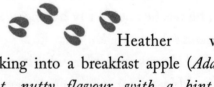Heather was actually just tucking into a breakfast apple (*Adam's Pearmain, sweet, nutty flavour with a hint of strawberries*) as she talked to Alastair and Rhona by the stile at the entrance to the tunnel.

'I think it's quite simple. Two of us go in and then one leads the chickens out, while the other encourages from the back.'

'I think you're nuts,' said Rhona in her most dismissive voice. 'Chickens are amazingly stupid.' She continued, 'You're never going to be able to persuade them to come and, even if you do, what'll happen to them when they get outside? Where will they go?'

'They'll be fine,' assured Heather. 'I mean, the wildcat obviously isn't going to eat them, is he? Any that don't know where to go can stay with us until they make plans.'

Alastair nodded. 'I can take them somewhere safe. I'll get Blackie to help, his paw's better now.'

Rhona was getting exasperated. 'What will they eat? Mr Busby will just round them all up and send them back. And it's his big healthy-eating event – there are loads of children and people all over the place. This is bonkers!'

But Heather wasn't to be stopped. 'If you'd seen what it's like down there you'd be on my side. Alastair, I think you'd better come in with me. I mean, you're a sheepdog, so you're probably better at herding than Rhona. You're certainly more patient!'

Rhona looked furious but she couldn't deny that was true.

From his vantage point in a nearby tree, Mr Hornbuckle watched his quarry. The moment she came close enough to the tree, he'd get her with his net. He tightened his grip on it so as to be ready. But yet again she surprised him. As he watched, the pig and the dog – neither species famous for being 'diggers' – disappeared into the ground, leaving the goat exactly where she was.

In the farmyard, things were getting busy. The children were being shown round the factory in groups and Isla's old class were up next. A big stage had been set up and there were journalists everywhere, even a local news camera.

'Come on, then,' called Mr Busby, as he welcomed the class into the factory.

It was the first time Isla had been into the barn since it had burned down and her eyes nearly popped out of her head. It was totally different. Machines everywhere, all steel and scrubbed floors, great rolls of plastic sheeting and piles and piles of the plastic trays to put the chickens in. At one end was a huge conveyor belt that seemed to come up from underground.

'Is that where you kill them?' asked Raj, pointing at the conveyor belt.

'It is, young man. Then they come up here to be packaged.'

'Is there loads of blood? Can we see?' added Jimmy Jamieson, going over to the conveyor belt.

'No!' shouted Mr Busby, running after the boy and grabbing him just as he was about to climb on the conveyor belt. 'No, it's not safe down there. No siree. No children allowed. Only, um, chickens. Right, now I think it's time for us to go outside and take some pictures.' Mr Busby ushered them all outside and went to close the factory door behind them.

As he did so, he heard something. It sounded like a dog barking, and it seemed to be coming from the basement. He cocked his head and listened, but there was only the noise coming from the children and the press outside. He must have been imagining things. Relieved, he went outside, closing the door behind him.

Heather had warned Alastair about the smell and what he was going to see, but even so, the sheepdog was utterly horrified when he followed her through the wall into the chicken barn. He barked with rage and indignation.

Mr Hornbuckle slid down from his tree and strode over to the hole where the pig and dog had disappeared. He shooed the goat away and very carefully peered down the hole. Then he took a camera and attached it to a small remote-controlled car. He synchronised the car with his smartphone and used the key pad to send it down the hole.

'Can you please all listen up?' Heather was addressing the chickens while Alastair stayed by the wall, trying not to breathe in the smell.

'We've come to get you out of here. We're going to go back down this tunnel and then you'll be free. If you could all get ready to, go we'll start moving you out.'

None of the chickens moved a muscle. They stayed exactly where they were and did nothing.

'Come on, everyone. If you could just form a line over here we'll get you through the tunnel as best we can.'

Nothing. The chickens looked at her like she was from another planet. Heather marched over to the liveliest looking one and looked her right in the eye.

'CAN-WE-GO-NOW-PLEASE?'

The chicken blinked at her. 'Is it time to go?'

Finally! 'Yes! Come on, don't be afraid – let's go.' Heather set off back towards the hole in the wall. When she got there she looked back, but none of them had moved.

'That's the wrong way. The factory's up there,' said the same one as before, gesturing with her head towards the conveyor belt.

Alastair couldn't hold his breath any longer. 'We're not taking you to the factory. We're escaping – you're going to be free!'

Nobody moved.

Heather didn't know what to do. How was she to get them to leave? At that moment, she heard a whirring noise coming from the tunnel. She ducked down to look through the hole in the wall and saw a strange thing on wheels coming towards her. She trotted up the tunnel to see what it was.

Mr Hornbuckle was watching the progress of the camera on his smartphone outside. He slid his fingers across the screen, inching the car slowly forward, and then, coming through the wall towards his camera, he saw a big, pink snout. It was Busby! As he watched, Busby's snout came up to the camera, stopped, sniffed it curiously and then gave it a prod with what looked like a trotter. Oh dear. He frantically tried to reverse, but it was too late. First the car was flipped onto its side, and then he heard a loud crunch and the screen went blank and fuzzy.

Heather lifted her bottom off the flattened car and walked back into the cellar. She turned to Alastair. 'Do you want to run up the tunnel and see if Rhona's okay?'

Alastair raced off and Heather turned back to the chickens. She walked over to one and stared at him.

'Please come with me.'

The chicken looked at Heather blankly, and opened its mouth to say something, but all that came out was a sort of sad, wailing sound.

At that momen,t Alastair raced back inside, his face looking grim.

'Rhona's gone and that man's there. I barked at him but he wasn't scared. Then he started coming down the tunnel.'

He looked over at the conveyor belt and then back at the motionless chickens. 'There's no way out. We're trapped.'

Chapter 17

'I Am Busby!'

Mr Hornbuckle was inching his way along the corridor towards the square of light he could see at the end. For a second, he felt as if he was back in the mine, chasing those pigs underground, and then he found the wreckage of his remote controlled car, lying on the ground where it had been squashed by Busby. He looked at it sadly and scrambled on faster.

Inside the factory, Heather was becoming frantic as she tried to get the chickens to move. 'Why won't you come with me? Don't you want to be free?'

The one who had been making the sad wailing noise looked at her curiously. 'Are you the farmer?'

It was like a light bulb going off over Heather's head. She rose up on her back trotters and cleared her throat. Then she shouted across the factory:

'Listen up, everyone! I'm Busby Pig, the farmer, and it's time to go to market. My friend Alastair is going to help you get up into the factory, so could you all please make your way over to the other side of the room?'

There was a low murmur of understanding and finally the chickens started to move. Taking care not to tread on any of them, Heather began putting them on the belt as Alastair ran to the control panel and pushed random buttons with his paws until the engine fired up and the conveyor belt started to move, taking the first of the chickens up to the factory above.

Mr Hornbuckle was shuffling along the tunnel, getting closer and closer to the hole in the wall. There was a very strong smell coming from the hole and he was having trouble getting his breath. Only a few more metres. He put his handkerchief over his nose and carried on.

Inside, there was now a constant stream of ill chickens going up the conveyor belt. Any that were too weak to get on were helped by Heather and, once they got through the trap door at the top, Alastair lifted them off the conveyor belt onto the stainless steel floor of the factory. It was taking a long time, though, and many of them were too weak to do anything. Heather herself had to do several rides up and down the belt with chickens hanging off her and riding on her back. The worst thing was all the ones that were being left behind, the poor chickens that either couldn't move at all or had died where they stood or sat.

Mr Hornbuckle scrambled the last few metres,

grabbed the wall and heaved himself through the hole, doing a commando roll to land inside the factory. The first thing he saw was Busby but, like Heather, it was the second thing he saw that would change his life for ever.

Heather was frantically loading the last lot of chickens onto the belt and preparing to get on herself, when she looked around and saw the most extraordinary sight. Mr Hornbuckle had emerged from the tunnel; but he wasn't looking at her, the escaping chickens, or even the conveyor belt. Instead, he was sitting in the middle of the floor, staring at the chickens who were too ill to move, with his head in his hands, tears streaming down his face.

Heather rode the conveyor belt upwards for the last time. When she got to the top she crawled through the machine into the factory and stood on top of the cold, grey machinery as she looked down at the wall-to-wall carpet of yellow chickens. The door was closed from the outside, no way through that. There were no windows, so that left only one thing to do. She picked up as many chickens as she could carry on her back, told any of them who could manage it to follow behind her, and started to climb.

Outside on the stage, Mr Busby was talking to the press about how free range and organic was the only way to raise chickens, when Isla suddenly pointed towards the barn and shouted, 'Look everyone – look up there!'

All eyes turned towards the barn, where they saw the most extraordinary sight. Standing at the top of the old barn, resplendent, and with the breeze ruffling her hair and the sun turning her into a flaming beacon, was none other than the original Busby pig.

'Busby!' everyone shouted and, thinking this was all part of the PR stunt, started taking photos and jostling to get the best position as they tried to see what was happening.

Only Mr Busby wasn't excited – in fact, he started to look very unhappy indeed, particularly when it became clear that Busby wasn't alone. One by one, and painfully slowly, chickens started to emerge from the air vent.

'It's Busby's chickens!' shouted the watching crowd, but soon the glee turned to confusion and then anger, as it started to dawn on people that these were not the lovely chickens who ran about the farmyard and featured in the photos on the packets and adverts for Busby's Birds. These were not free-range chickens, bursting with health and life, but sad, corpulent, flaccid chickens. Chickens who tried to fly off the roof but were so weak and weighed down by their overweight bodies they simply fell to the ground. Chickens who hadn't lived any of their lives in farmyards, and certainly hadn't been bred by a caring farmer like Busby the pig.

The photographers were clicking away frantically as Mr Busby picked up one of the chickens which had fallen down from the roof, and held it up.

'You see, these are exactly the sort of chickens you

will *never* find on a Busby's Birds farm. I'm glad you've enjoyed the presentation – now let's go over to the farmhouse office, and I can talk you all through the future development plans for Busby's Birds.'

He started trying to lead the journalists away, but they were all far too interested in Busby up on the roof and were still snapping away. Desperate to get her down, Mr Busby picked up a stone and hurled it at her. It bounced off the roof and he grabbed another and another.

'Stop!' shouted Isla, as a stone hit her friend, followed by another one.

Heather tried to get back into the air duct, but it was blocked with chickens. As Mr Busby picked up a large rock and took aim, Isla knew she had to do something.

She jumped up and shouted at the top of her voice, 'Old Meldrum Primary! Charge!' and she raced towards the barn.

She was immediately followed by a stream of children. Mr Busby tried to stop them but he was engulfed as they flooded over him, flattening him as they charged at the factory door, pushing and pushing, but to no avail. As Mr Busby got to his feet, shouting, 'Stop them!' a voice whispered in Isla's ear, 'Try this,' and a hand gave her a key. Isla grabbed it, unlocked the doors and pushed, but they wouldn't move – in fact, they started to open outwards. Even the crowd of children were powerless to resist as the doors swung open and a river of chickens burst out, pushing the doors wide and flooding them and the farmyard in a torrent of yellow fluffiness.

It was mayhem. Alastair and Nikki's dog Izzy were barking, the children were whooping, and camera flashbulbs were frantically popping. Everyone was taking pictures of all the birds as they came pouring out of the barn, in a never-ending stream of yellow and white. Some of them were not really able to walk but were carried along by the others, unable to stop themselves as they were pushed along from behind. Then some of them started trying to fly and some succeeded, and within minutes it was as if the whole farmyard had been painted yellow and filled with fluffy balloons as chickens went everywhere and feathers flew in the air. Mr Busby rushed frantically around, trying hopelessly to catch them and put them all back into the barn, before giving up and sitting on the ground, head in his hands as chickens clambered all over him, pecking at him crossly, almost as if they knew he was responsible for their misery.

Where was Heather? Isla was frantically looking around but she couldn't see her friend anywhere. Then she was caught up in the mayhem and madness as a chicken half flew up and flopped onto her head before sliding down onto the ground.

In the midst of all this, a figure emerged from the barn, strode through the crowd and hauled Mr Busby to his feet. It was Horatio Hornbuckle, and he was furious. 'Mr Busby, I am arresting you in my capacity as a Pest Control Operative. You are charged with gross and appalling mistreatment of animals, fraud, and false advertising.' He produced a pair of handcuffs from his pocket and, to the accompaniment of more flashing cameras, he led a plucked and sorry Mr Busby away to his waiting car.

Mr Wolstenholme and Nikki were laughing and

trying to avoid treading on stray chickens, as Isla went over and handed Nikki the key to the factory.

'Is this yours?'

As Nikki grinned at her, Isla pointed to where Mr Busby was being shoved into Mr Hornbuckle's car. 'He's going to be really cross with you for giving me that key.'

Nikki smiled and gave her a wink. 'Oh! I had no idea. I thought it was for your bedroom.' Then she glanced behind Isla. 'I think somebody wants you.'

Isla spun round. It was Rhona the goat, pulling at her sleeve and leading her round the back of the barn.

Rhona stopped and tapped her hoof until Isla sat down. Then she trotted off and came back with three sticks, which she laid out on the ground. As Isla watched in amazement, Rhona started to scrape her hoof in the earth, almost as if she was drawing something. She drew for a while and then, when she was done, she came over to Isla and grabbed her sleeve again. Isla got up and walked over to where Rhona had drawn in the earth.

The three sticks had been made into a crude arrow,

pointing towards the tractor barn, but the extraordinary thing was what was underneath. It wasn't a drawing, it was writing. Two words, in fact. They were scraped by a hoof, they were wobbly and shaky, but they were definitely words and they had been written by a goat.

HEAT   HER

Isla studied the words, very puzzled. 'Heat her? Heat who? I don't understand.'

Rhona looked at her, and Isla could have sworn the goat was cross. She felt like she did when she couldn't solve a maths question and her teacher looked at her with a patient but slightly disappointed expression on her face.

Then Mr Le Four appeared, looking a bit dazed. He peered over Isla's shoulder.

'You found her, then?'

Isla didn't understand. 'I'm sorry?'

The teacher pointed at the words on the ground. 'Your friend. Heather.'

Isla clapped her hands and cheered. It wasn't two words at all. It was one. *Heat her* was Heather! She shouted, 'Heather!' at the top of her voice and could have sworn the goat smiled at her. Then, as Isla thanked the bemused Mr Le Four, Rhona butted her towards a tunnel under the tractor barn.

Slightly nervously, Isla got into the tunnel and started to crawl. She only went about three metres before she emerged into a sort of nest, full of straw, half eaten books, and three pigs. Heather was lying on her side, looking absolutely exhausted but very happy and, beside her, snuggled in and suckling frantically, were two brand new piglets. A bright red Duroc boy and, next to him, a little, stripy, bearded piglet girl. Isla burst into floods of tears and threw herself around the neck of her best animal friend ever. They'd been separated, come back together and then separated once more, but this time Isla was determined they would never be apart again.

The End

Appleogue

Now that Mr Busby had been exposed as a liar, Busby's Birds went bankrupt and the farm went up for sale. Heather took Isla to the ruin and together they dug up the sword and coins Heather had found. It was the Laird Angus Gordon's sword, hidden over two hundred and fifty years before, so it was a genuine Jacobite relic and, together with the coins, worth quite a lot. They gave the coins and the sword to the museum and used the reward money to buy back the farm. Isla kept one of the coins and turned it into a matching necklace for Heather.

The funny thing was that the medlar tree started growing leaves again, and next autumn, it was absolutely groaning with fruit. Every year after that it produced amazing blossom and an incredible amount of fruit, almost as if it were making up for lost time. Mr Wolstenholme said it was probably because the metal from the sword had been poisoning the roots and stopping the fruit growing, but Isla knew it was because the ghost had finally made amends and the curse was lifted. Either way, Mr Wolstenholme used the fruit to make jam and started a new business called 'Jacobite Jellies' which he ran from the factory where the chickens had once been imprisoned.

Nikki stayed to help run the business, so that meant that her dog Izzy and Alastair could be friends as well.

The rabbits soon became healthy again, and Mr

Wolstenholme pulled down all the huge fences that had ringed the farm. Strangely, despite the farm being all open and unprotected, not a single one of Isla's chickens was taken. Heather never saw the wildcat again, but she suspected this was his way of showing her she'd earned his respect.

Mr Hornbuckle finally got to take a Busby back to London – even if it was the man, not the pig – and he was so appalled by what he'd seen in Mr Busby's barn that he gave up being a pest control operative and now works for the government as a chicken farm inspector. Nobody can quite understand why he keeps a toy pig on his desk.

Rhona started to teach herself Spanish. '*Yo soy una cabra, y me gusta comer libros.*' One of the first things she discovered was that 'Eder' is a real Basque name, and it means 'pretty'.

Alastair and Izzy had a lot of puppies very fast so, what with the piglets, who Heather called Aitor and Eder, suddenly the farm seems full of youngsters and very alive again – particularly when Thom and Ramelan stop by on their annual migration north, and stay for a few days. The other four pigs all handed themselves in and were returned to London Zoo, but the 'wild piglets' are determined to stay wild for as long as they can. So, if you're ever in Sherwood Forest and they steal your bread, keep it to yourself!

When her piglets ask about their father, Heather sits them down and tells them the amazing stories he used to tell her. She tells them how wise he was, how knowledgeable, how annoying, and how brave. She sent Thom and Ramelan to look for him once, but they said the mine was empty. There was no sign of him.

'Do you think he escaped? Will he come and find us, Mum?'

'You never can tell, little Eder, you never can tell.'

And what about Heather? She's getting on a bit now; she spends quite a lot of time sitting on her own and thinking about things quietly. She doesn't mind thinking these days, in fact, she told Rhona she thought she was getting rather good at it.

She still sees Isla masses, although the little girl is

in big school now and spends quite a lot of time talking on her phone, a funny flat black thing that Heather only trusts because it has a picture of an apple on it.

So it was an extra treat the other day when Heather was fast-trotting (it was lunchtime) round the back of the barn and saw the familiar sight of two legs sticking out of the barn, bent at the knees so the feet stuck up, the scuffed boots crossed at the ankle as they jiggled back and forth. As she got nearer she heard the unmistakable sound of Isla's voice, bubbling like a stream, and she cautiously slowed down so as not to break the spell.

'. . . can you believe it? She knew he'd stolen the chicken and so she charged, right at him! How brave is that?'

Heather peered round the corner of the barn and saw a sight that made her heart flip right over. Isla was lying flat on her tummy, facing two little piglets, one red, one striped, both motionless apart from their wiggling tails, and both gazing at the girl adoringly, as Isla's voice held them completely transfixed, just as it had done their mother for nearly fourteen years . . .

'. . . I tell you what, guys, and I mean this in the best way possible, your mum, she's . . . immense . . .'

Heather scrunched.

Have you read all of Heather's amazing adventures?

  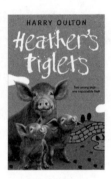

Available from all good bookshops and in ebook

Find out more at

www.piccadillypress.co.uk